FRESH AS A

DAISY

THE LILLYMOUTH MYSTERIES

BOOK ONE

R. A. Hutchins

ISBN: 9798374796766

For Michael, I can't wait to write more chapters with you! All my love xx

Other Murder Mystery Titles by this Author:

Baker's Rise Mysteries -
Here Today, Scone Tomorrow
Pie Comes Before A Fall
Absence Makes the Heart Grow Fondant
Muffin Ventured, Muffin Gained
Out with the Old, In with the Choux
All's Fair in Loaf and War
A Walk In the Parkin
The Jam Before the Storm
Things Cannoli Get Better (May 2023)

CAST OF CHARACTERS

ARCHIE – Mynah bird

CATHY BARNES – Local baker

STAN BARNES – Local baker

DAISY BLOOM – New parish vicar

WENDY BLOOM (DECEASED) – Daisy's grandmother

COUNCILLOR BARRY BRIDGES – Local councillor

MARTHA BRIDGES – Wife of local councillor, on parish council

LIZZIE BRIGGS (DECEASED) – Sister of Robert Briggs Senior

ROBERT BRIGGS SENIOR – Local landowner of Briggs' Farm

ROB (ROBERT) BRIGGS JUNIOR – Son of Robert Briggs Senior

GERALD BUNCH – Local florist

RON CARMICHAEL (DECEASED) – Sylvia's husband

SYLVIA CARMICHAEL – Wendy Bloom's best friend

DETECTIVE INSPECTOR RHYS CLUERO – Local detective

NORA CLUMPING – Vicarage housekeeper

GEMMA DALTON (NEE SANDERSON) – Co-owner of local pub, the Crow's Nest Inn

PAUL DALTON – Gemma's husband, works at Briggs' Farm

ANDREW FREEMAN – Bea's husband, joiner

BEA (ABIGAIL) FREEMAN – Owner of Bea's Book Nook and Daisy's best friend

DAISY MAE FREEMAN – Daughter of Bea and Andrew, Daisy's goddaughter

ANTHONY GLENDINNING – Son of Violet and Percy

PERCY GLENDINNING – Local bank manager

VIOLET GLENDINNING – Wife of Percy, head of parish council

DANIEL HARPER – Bea's dad

MORAG HARPER – Bea's mum

JACOB – Vicarage cat

BUGSY MALONE – Sylvia's house rabbit

REVEREND MARTIN – Daisy's predecessor

DETECTIVE INSPECTOR MICHELLE MATLOCK – Local detective

JOE (JOSEPH) PIERCE – Café owner at 'The Boatyard'

BILLY SANDERSON – Co-owns the Crow's Nest Inn with his daughter Gemma.

ARTHUR SMITH – Church Handyman

MILDRED SPRATT – Church organist

LYDIA STANLEY – Works in planning department at local council offices

ROSEMARY WESSEX – Local librarian

CONTENTS

1. YOU CANNOT FIGHT GRAVITY

Readjusting the old cricket hat which was doing only a marginal job of keeping the sun's harsh glare from his eyes, Arthur Smith shifted his weight on the top rung of the wooden church ladder. His spare hand was planted firmly on the roof, just above the guttering, to keep him steady while he worked. Right now, though, having just repositioned the two loose tiles that were the purpose of his climb, Arthur was taking a breather and enjoying the scenery.

From this high vantage point he could take in his favourite view in the world – the whole town of Lillymouth lay before him. From the old main street of Cobble Wynd to his left, still home to many of the local shops, down to the town square and from there to the park and then to the promenade and beach which bordered Lillywater Bay. Looking straight across, the main square was framed on the church side by the small cottages of Broad Street and opposite, by the tall four-story townhouses of The Parade. Then came the Lillywater river which flowed into the harbour and out to sea between the twin piers. Beyond that the fields of Bayview Farm on the right and the old train station on the left. If you travelled another few miles south across country, you would eventually reach the north Yorkshire moors in all their stark glory.

Arthur had fond memories set in every part of this place. From playing pirates in the coastal caves as a boy, to the time the teenage version of himself thought it would be a good idea if he and a few of his friends 'borrowed' a fishing boat and went for a day trip across the Bay to Smugglers' Isle. Of course, now well into his sixties those days of uninhibited adventuring were in the dim and distant past. But he still often ventured into the wilds of the moors, enjoying the solitude and familiarity of the place. In fact, in recent times, heavy of heart and with some new discoveries to ponder, Arthur had been escaping to the land of gorse and heather much more regularly.

Dragging himself from his reminiscences, and from the

view which was his happy place, Arthur double-checked the tiles around him, almost regretful that the job hadn't been a bigger one. The new vicar was arriving today, and Arthur had to admit he wasn't keen to meet them. Certainly not if they were anything like their predecessor. No, he would rather hide up here all day if possible. Arthur tried to shake off the dark thoughts that threatened to infiltrate the pure joy that the outlook from up here gave him. At the top of this ladder, perched on the roof of the Church of St. John the Baptist, Arthur found a peace that ordinarily eluded him.

Nevertheless, return to reality he must. Nora would have his hide if he didn't do the weeding at the vicarage before the new incumbent made their appearance.

Sighing, Arthur readjusted the foot that had remained on the top rung of the ladder, checking his hold before beginning his slow descent – made slower nowadays by the arthritis in his aging knees. Happy that it was safe, he went to move his other leg into position, only for the whole top half of the extendable, wooden ladder to judder beneath him.

"What the..?" Arthur asked aloud. The ladder was old, he knew, but just like him the dependable object had plenty of good days left in it still. They didn't make things to last these days – it was one of Arthur's favourite bugbears.

As the whole wooden structure began to sway dangerously, with Arthur perched on top of it, gripping to the sides in desperate confusion, his hat took flight and sailed off down to the graveyard below. Allowing himself to lean over slightly, to try to find the cause of the unexpected momentum, Arthur saw his cricket cap amongst the overgrown grass between the headstones – something which was next on his list of tasks after weeding, Arthur recalled. He did enjoy mowing though…

Distracted by the thought, and by the swaying motion that was starting to make him feel slightly seasick, Arthur didn't see the figure until they stepped out of the deep shadows which clung to the church wall on this side. That he was surprised to see the person was one thing, but Arthur was more concerned about the tight grip their gloved hands had on the bottom of his ladder.

"Oh hello," Arthur called in their direction, "I can make my own way down, thanks, no need to hold the ladder for me."

For the briefest of moments their eyes met and, had his

situation not been already so precarious, Arthur would have been knocked backwards by the sheer amount of malice he saw there.

"Oy! Hold on!" He shouted, louder this time, as he felt the ladder being pulled away from the roof, away from the side of the church building altogether. Still swaying, he was now tipped backwards to such an angle, that Arthur knew deep in his gut what the inevitable outcome of his position would be – you cannot fight gravity, after all.

It all happened so fast, and yet so ridiculously slowly, one minute he was falling backwards through the air, still clinging to the stupid ladder which was plastered to his front. The next, Arthur crashed into the small cemetery, his neck and the back of his skull making harsh contact with a moss-covered headstone.

"What a terrible accident," the onlooker said, checking to ensure Arthur's pulse was silent before they removed their gloves and walked away with a new jaunt to their step.

2. SEEK YE FIRST

Daisy Bloom hummed along to the Abba song on Smooth radio, pondering how she might use the lyric 'knowing me, knowing you' this coming Sunday, in the first sermon she would deliver in her new parish. She was barely concentrating on her driving in fact, knowing the roads like the back of her hand as she did. Barely anything changed around here, in this small coastal corner of Yorkshire, and Daisy really wasn't sure if that was a good thing or not. It had been fifteen years since she had left the town of Lillymouth, at the tender age of eighteen, and the newly ordained vicar had not been back since. Indeed, had the Bishop himself not personally decreed this was the parish for her – in some misguided attempt to help her chase away the demons of her past, Daisy presumed – then she suspected that she would not have come back now either.

Positives, think about the positives, Daisy told herself, pushing a finger between her dog collar and her neck to let a bit of air in. The weather was remarkably lovely for early July in the North of England, and Daisy was regretting wearing the item which designated her as a member of the clergy. She had wanted to arrive at her new vicarage with no possibility that they not immediately recognise her as the new incumbent – after that awful time when she turned up as the curate of her last parish, and they had mistaken her as the new church cleaner – she knew she looked very different from the fresh-faced girl who had left town under a black cloud, so there was a good chance even the older townsfolk wouldn't recognise her.

Anyway, positive thoughts, positive thoughts, Daisy allowed her mind to wander to the shining light, the beacon of hope for her return to this little town – her new goddaughter and namesake, Daisy Mae, daughter of her best friend from high school, Bea. Pulling up outside of the bookshop which her friend owned, and glad to have found a disabled parking spot so close, Daisy was surprised to find she was relieved that the old Victorian building had not changed since she left all those years ago. It still stood tall and proud on the bottom corner of Cobble Wynd and Front Street, it's wooden façade hinting at its age. The building had been a bookshop since Edwardian times, Daisy knew, and she smiled as she saw the window display was filled with baby books and toys – old and new coming together in harmony, something that, according to the Bishop, was far from happening in the town as a whole.

"Daisy!" the familiar voice brought a sudden lump to her throat as Daisy made her way into the relative dimness of the shop, the smell of books and coffee a welcome comfort. The voice of the woman who had been her childhood friend, who had been one of the few to support her when the worst happened all those years ago… *positive thoughts…*

"Bea," Daisy leant her walking stick against the old wooden counter and reached out to hug her friend, careful that her own ample bosom didn't squash the little baby that was held in a carrier at her mother's chest. Wanting to say more, but finding herself unable to speak around her emotion, Daisy tried to put all of the love and affection she could into that physical touch.

"Meet Daisy Mae," Bea said proudly, pulling back and turning sideways so that Daisy could see the baby's face.

"The photos didn't do her justice, Bea, really, she's beautiful." Okay, now the feelings had gone to her eyes, and Daisy tried to wipe them discreetly with the back of her hand. She wasn't this person, who was so easily moved – or at least she hadn't been since she ran and left Lillymouth behind. Daisy had funded herself through training and then worked as a police support officer for victims of violence for almost a decade, before hearing the calling to serve a higher purpose. She had survived assault and injury as part of her previous profession, seen some truly horrible things, and yet had not felt as emotional as she did now. Not since the day she quit this place, in fact…

"Aw, you must be tired from the drive," Bea, tactful and sensitive as always, gave her the perfect 'out', "come and have a cuppa and a sandwich in the tea nook. Andrew just finished refurbishing it for me."

"Thank you, but let me get it for you, are you even meant to be working so soon after the birth?"

"I'm just covering lunchtimes while my maternity cover nips out for a quick bite – well, I think she's actually meeting her boyfriend, she never manages to stick to just the one hour, but, ah, she's young and well read… why don't you hold little Daisy Mae while I get us sorted with something?"

"Oh! I… well, I…"

"You'll be fine, Daisy, you're going to have a lot of babies to hold during christenings, you know! I can't wait for you to christen this little one," Bea chuckled and unfastened the baby pouch, handing the now squirming bundle to the vicar without hesitation once Daisy had lowered herself into a squashy leather armchair.

Wide, deep blue eyes, the colour of the swell in Lillywater Bay on a stormy day, looked up at Daisy with surprise and she found herself saying a quick prayer that the baby wouldn't start to scream. Daisy desperately wanted to be a part of this little girl's life, feeling as she did that she might never have a child of her own. What she had seen in her previous profession had put Daisy off relationships for life. As part of the Church of England she was not forbidden from getting married and starting a family – quite the opposite – but Daisy's own feelings on the matter ran deep and dark.

"Here we go," Bea returned with a tray holding a pot of tea, two china mugs, a plate of sandwiches and some cakes, "you look like you could do with this."

"You aren't wrong there," Daisy felt suddenly and surprisingly bereft as baby Daisy Mae was lifted gently from her arms and placed in a pram in the corner next to them.

"Have you visited the vicarage yet? Nora will be on tenterhooks waiting for you, she'll have Arthur fixing and cleaning everything, poor man!"

"I haven't had that pleasure," Daisy smiled ruefully, "I thought I'd come to visit my two favourites first." Daisy knew she was being slightly cowardly, but Nora Clumping was not a woman to become reacquainted with on an empty stomach. She had been the housekeeper at the vicarage for as long as Daisy could remember, surviving numerous clergy, and she had seemed ancient to Daisy as a girl. She could only imagine how old the woman must be now. She must have a soft side though, Daisy had thought to herself on the journey from Leeds, otherwise she wouldn't have taken Arthur in decades ago and adopted him as her own. Not that that diminished from the woman's formidable presence, however… for someone so slight in stature, she was certainly a powerhouse to contend with!

"Ah, wise choice," Bea agreed, "and if I were you, I'd pick up some fruit scones from Barnes the Baker's before you head up there!"

"Sound advice," Daisy laughed out loud, before remembering the baby who had now fallen back asleep, and lowered her voice to a whisper to joke, "I may be in the church now, but I'm not above the odd bit of bribery where necessary!"

"Just wait till you hear her views on the previous vicar," Bea said, not a small amount of excitement in her voice, "oh how I wish I could be a fly on the wall!"

"Argh," Daisy groaned exaggeratedly into her coffee mug causing her friend to snort.

"I want all the details afterwards," Bea continued, "I'll bet you five pounds that within ten minutes she mentions that time she caught you making a daisy chain with flowers you'd pulled from the vicarage garden."

"I was eight!" Daisy replied in mock protest, even while still knowing her friend was right – nothing was ever forgotten in small towns like these.

"Well, I've still got your back like I did then," Bea said, reaching over to rub Daisy's shoulder conspiratorially, and adding with a wink, "and I'm sure she isn't allowed to give the new vicar chores as punishment!"

Perhaps coming back to this place after so long won't be so bad after all, Daisy thought. *With good friends like this, I can serve the parish, find the justice I seek for Gran and be out of here before the Bishop can say 'Amen.'*

The Bible says 'seek ye first the Kingdom of God' – well, I've done that, now I can seek out a cold hearted killer. They may have gotten away with it for over a decade, but divine retribution is about to be served.

3. A BUNCH OF BLOOMS

Cobble Wynd, where the baker's, butcher's and other similar shops were still to be found, was a pedestrian-only zone which Daisy didn't feel she had the strength to navigate today. Even on a dry day, it would be a tricky walk for her, owing to the cobbles which gave it its name, and also the fact that the street was on a hill. So, she drove along Broad Street and cut up past the parish hall to Church Street. Not wanting to continue to the church and vicarage just yet, and announce her presence without the peace offering her friend had suggested, Daisy parked discreetly behind the hall and from there it was only a two minute walk onto the main shopping street of the small town.

"Well I never, you're a blast from the past to be sure," Cathy Barnes – or rather, a greyer, rounder version of the woman Daisy had known growing up – rushed from behind the counter to welcome her like a long-lost friend, hugging Daisy closely to her and causing the vicar to wince from the pain that shot down her back and leg. Her cane clattered to the floor, and Daisy bit down on the rather ungodly words which formed on her tongue.

Cathy stepped back to see the cause of the noise, and immediately raised an enquiring eyebrow at the offending article, which Daisy was now struggling to pick up, "Here, let me get that for you lass."

"Thank you, Cathy," a small silence ensued which was anything but comfortable, the other woman obviously waiting for an explanation as to Daisy's need for such an implement.

When none was forthcoming, however, she simply continued as if nothing had happened, much to Daisy's own relief, "And look at you with your dog collar and everything, all grown up. I couldn't half believe it when Nora told me who the new reverend was. I remember the little girl who loved my iced buns, running across from her grandma's shop to buy one with her pennies – oh sorry, love, maybe I shouldn't have mentioned her when you're just back…"

"No, no it's fine Cathy, really. There are memories of

Gran all around here, I won't be able to avoid them, as much as I may want to," Daisy wished she'd engaged her filter, but the truth was the truth and she aimed to start out as she meant to go on.

"Aye well, may she rest in peace, lovely woman that she was. Awful business, just awful, ah… So, what can I do for you today, lass?"

"Three of your famous fruit scones please, Cathy – and do you still stock the fruit jam from Briggs up at Bayview farm? And the clotted cream?" As nothing in the small shop seemed to have changed in her absence, Daisy guessed she was safe to assume their food offering would have also remained the same. It still smelled of freshly baked bread, still had the faded, old posters from times gone by in frames on the wall behind the counter, still felt like a treat. Daisy had to silently shake herself to not get caught up in the exact memories she was trying to avoid.

"I do lass, aye, though there's been some goings on up there…" as if checking herself, Cathy let her sentence trail off, shrugging her shoulders, and busied herself behind the counter.

"I imagine there is a lot to catch up on in the past decade and a half," Daisy helped her out, "you'll have to come round to the vicarage for tea – you and Stan –

and tell me all about it, when I'm settled in."

"I'd like that, love," Cathy looked like she was about to say something else too, but at that moment the bell above the door rang and a tall, thin man entered. His jet black hair was greased sideways across his crown, over wide, hooded eyes that seemed out of proportion on his thin face, which ended in a pointed chin covered in straggly hairs. For some reason, he reminded Daisy of a crow, or even better, a Billy goat and she had to stop herself from both giggling and staring.

The new customer had definitely clocked the vicar and he certainly did not share her politeness, however, as a narrow, pointed tongue darted out and he began licking his lips in such a slow motion whilst staring intently at her bosom. Despite wanting desperately to look away, Daisy found herself transfixed on the uncouth arrival.

Cathy, too, watched the man with an overt look of distaste, before obviously catching herself staring and saying, "Daisy Bloom, meet Gerald Bunch, owner of your Gran's sho… ah, of the florist's."

"Daisy Bloom!" The voice which Daisy had for some reason expected to be thin and tinny, was in fact a low, booming sound which almost rattled the glass front of the cake counter in front of them, "Bloom and Bunch!

Ha ha, I bet we could make a gorgeous bunch of blooms! You're not married are you?" He stared at Daisy's left hand intently, until she recovered from her shock at his statement, and at the lascivious wink which followed, and realised the man was looking for a wedding band.

"Well, I…" she pointed ineffectually at her dog collar, as if this might offer some kind of divine protection from the man's lecherous remarks.

Not put off in the slightest, he continued, "We could make a blooming pair, ha ha, have a bunch of fun…"

"Anyway," Cathy spoke over the odious man, "here you go, Vicar," she placed particular emphasis on that last word, and glared at her fellow shopkeeper.

"Thank you, how much…"

"Consider it a welcome home present, lass."

Home. Was this home? It had been once… Daisy thought as she thanked the kind woman and tried to squeeze herself back out of the shop without touching the man who refused to budge out of her way, as if he was taking pleasure in her nearness and in seeing her squirm.

"Eugh," Daisy spoke aloud as she finally freed herself

of the enclosed space and took great gulpfuls of the salty sea air that always permeated the town.

Tempted as she was to walk the few feet across the lane to look in the window of the flower shop that had once been her home, Daisy forced herself to go back to her car, her gait now a distinctive limp from having been on her feet for so long. She was more than ready to arrive at her new lodgings, to take her time unpacking the car and enjoying a cup of Earl Grey in the peace of the vicarage garden.

You'd think she'd have learnt by now, though, that sometimes God has other plans.

4. THE PROFESSIONALS HAVE WORK TO DO

Daisy heard the sirens before she saw the emergency vehicles themselves, the all-too familiar din causing the hairs on the back of her neck to bristle and a tremor to run though her body.

They're not here for Gran this time, or for me for that matter. I'm also no longer responsible for helping the victims find refuge and pick up their lives… she reassured herself as the vicar edged gingerly onto her car seat, trying desperately not to aggravate the pain in her side further. *Though they do seem awfully close.*

She wasn't wrong, as when Daisy attempted to drive through the large, wrought iron gates which opened from Church Street and onto the driveway – which ordinarily led past the church and graveyard and up to the tiny vicarage cottage – she found her way blocked by two police cars. Looking past them, she saw an ambulance parked straddling the footpath next to the church building itself.

Reversing slightly, and sending a prayer heavenward for whomever required such emergency attention, Daisy parked back on the street and slowly left the safety of her own vehicle. Her heart hammered in her chest and her breathing came in short gasps, as she tried to rein in her anxious response to the unexpected situation.

Get a grip! You've been to scenes like this dozens of times, Daisy mentally chastised herself, stopping to talk to the rather surly-looking police officer who was stationed at the gates. She hadn't managed to get a word out, though, before the man levelled her with a distinctly bored gaze.

"No visitors today," he spoke gruffly before turning immediately away again.

"Actually, I'm the new vicar," Daisy forced herself to speak with confidence and assurance, the way she always had before her assault.

The man turned back slowly, as if he really didn't have a care in the world, flicked an invisible piece of lint from his uniform and studied her from head to toe, making a point of lingering on Daisy's dog collar before speaking again, "Hmm," was all he said, leaving Daisy none the wiser as to whether she was to be allowed past him.

The man turned his back to her, causing the hairs on Daisy's neck to bristle in anger this time, as she was effectively dismissed until she heard him speaking into his radio. Indistinct mumbling followed, from which the vicar could discern nothing of the conversation, until at length the officer turned back to her, "Aye you can go on up, it's not a pretty sight mind."

"Thank you," Daisy strode past with a force that belied both her physical pain and her emotional trauma, her stick hitting the gravelled ground with a repetitive thud. She threaded her way between the two police cars and then squashed past the ambulance, having to stumble on through the overgrown grass of the cemetery to do so, coming to a sudden halt when she saw the taped-off scene before her, of blood-splattered stone and grass. No human form was visible, thank goodness, and Daisy hoped they were getting attention in the ambulance.

"What the heck are you doing here?" A sharp voice from behind caused Daisy to pivot on her good leg. Inhaling slowly to regulate her breathing, the vicar's eyes met those that she had hoped never to see again. "Daisy Bloom! Well I never! Talk about an unwelcome blast from the past – still sticking your nose where it's not wanted, I see!"

"Hello Michelle, it's actually Reverend Bloom now," Daisy held her own as she came face to face with the girl – now a woman – who had bullied her mercilessly throughout high school.

"And it's Detective Inspector Matlock to you," the broad woman, dressed in a tight black suit, barked back, casting a disdainful glare towards Daisy's dog collar and then down to her walking stick, the sight of which made her mouth twist into an unkind smile, "now scuttle on off, there's a good girl, none of this is your concern. The professionals have work to do here, though I doubt a crime has even been committed. Stupid old sod probably just lost his balance."

"Actually, this is my parish now, and anything that happens on this church-owned land is very much my concern," Daisy stood her ground, affecting the stony expression which had given nothing away when violent partners had come looking for their victims in her past life.

They stood glaring at one another, neither willing to back down, until eventually the detective turned to walk away, throwing one final remark over her shoulder, "Well don't get in anyone's way or I'll have you out on your ear – you and that meddling housekeeper."

"Ignore her, lass," the familiar voice came from the direction of the vicarage and Daisy automatically turned towards it.

"Mrs. Clumping," Daisy hobbled forward, unable to move with ease now.

"Call me Nora, Vicar, and let me have a look at you lass. How long has it been? Ten, eleven years?"

"Fifteen," Daisy reached the woman, who was a shell of the strong, hard-nosed version she remembered. This lady was very old, slight and hunched, the skin on her face so paper thin that it was almost transparent – seemingly so fragile that she would topple sideways if you blew on her.

"Goodness, well, I was hoping to welcome you back with a special lunch and to catch you up on all the news around here, but as you can see…" Nora trailed off, and her eyes filled with unshed tears. Had it been anyone else, Daisy may have reached out to embrace them, but she knew that Nora Clumping had never been a hugger.

"Oh Nora, come on let's get you inside, and you can tell me all about it," Daisy was desperate to see what – or who – the bulk of the ambulance had been hiding from her view, praying that their injuries were not too serious, though the mere presence of detectives would seem to dispel that theory. The woman in front of her needed Daisy's attention more in this moment, however. That was what she told herself, anyway – it had nothing to do with not wanting to anger a certain detective... old habits, old responses died hard, it seemed, and Daisy tried to shake off the feelings of fear, inadequacy and of being the odd one out that the chance encounter had provoked.

"Aye lass, tis awful, really," Nora lurched forwards as they entered the cool, dim hallway and Daisy was grateful to get out of the heat and away from prying eyes, grabbing hold of the housekeeper's elbow and steadying her until she could grasp the door frame.

Having never seen the Nora Clumping of old show any emotion other than annoyance or apparent apathy, Daisy knew she would have to rely on her ecclesiastical training to overcome her own emotions and help the woman through whatever this incident was.

"He's dead and they won't let me near him," it was said so quietly, in such an emotionless tone, that for a moment Daisy was unsure if she had heard correctly.

"Who's dead, Nora?" A familiar churning began in Daisy's stomach, as if her body couldn't bear to hear the news. Coupled with an awful sense of déjà-vu, Daisy found herself pitching forwards onto the nearest kitchen chair.

"My Arthur!"

5. THAT'S NEW

"Arthur? Dead?" Daisy parroted the words back as if her voice was on autopilot. Certainly, her brain was having a hard time computing the new information, made all the more difficult by the siren noise that seemed to have permeated the thick stone walls of the old cottage. "How can it be so loud in here?" Daisy asked herself under her breath.

Nora's hearing was till as sharp as ever, however, as the older woman replied, "Oh that's Archie, or The Archbishop of York as he likes to call himself."

"Archie?" Daisy asked, wondering if this was another down-on-their-luck neighbour whom the vicarage housekeeper had taken under her wing.

"Aye lass, awful bird he is, always imitating things and

giving me a splitting headache. I'd have given him to the rescue shelter the day the last curate left him behind, 'cept that Arthur had a soft spot for the mangy thing. Any animals in fact, even those pesky pigeons roosting in the church spire." At the mention of the man who had been the closest thing to family the woman had had for many decades, the tears threatening to spill out from Nora's eyes finally won the battle. She swiped at them with gnarly knuckles, refusing to let the treacherous wetness reach her chin.

It was that sight that tipped Daisy into a full-blown panic attack.

The vicar couldn't remember the last time she had felt the all-too familiar tightening of her chest and rush of blood in her ears. The feeling that she couldn't breathe in deeply enough to take a full breath, that she might die from the lack of oxygen to muscles that were painfully tight.

In the years after her grandmother's murder, and again after the assault that had left her handicapped, Daisy had taken anti-depressants to keep a lid on the anxious thoughts and feelings that assailed her without warning. It had been years now, though, since she had weaned herself off that medication, making the current feeling of panic all the more terrifying. Too consumed by the experience to even feel embarrassed, Daisy clutched one hand to her chest, trying to count backwards from ten to slow her breathing and resume some semblance of control over her body. She was unaware of Nora rubbing her back, or even of the glass of water that was placed in her shaking hand, until a giant ball of orange fur jumped into Daisy's lap, effectively pinning her to the chair and providing a much-needed sense of connection with her environment.

"Jacob! Jacob! Get off her!" Daisy heard Nora's urgent whisper, "Let the girl breathe!"

"No," the single word caught in her dry throat, forcing Daisy to try again, "no, Nora, he's okay, thank you, I... I needed something to ground me."

"Aye well, he's a big lump that's for sure, I'm shocked he's been useful," Nora replied, though Daisy caught the indulgent half smile the woman directed towards the hefty creature currently massaging her thigh with his treading claws. The small pinpricks of pain were enough to keep Daisy distracted and allow her breathing to return to normal. Not normally a fan of animals, completely unable to see the attraction, in fact, Daisy was grateful for the cat in that moment, even if he merely seemed to view her as a cushy spot on which to nap. Thankfully the ghastly bird, who must be in the hallway Daisy presumed, had ceased his imitation of the emergency services, and a momentary calm returned to the small house.

Daisy and Nora simply looked at each other in horrified silence, both with red-rimmed eyes and blotchy cheeks.

"We'll be needing a pot of tea," Nora said, standing to the loud protestation of her joints. All sign of weakness, of emotion, was once again hidden behind her hard façade, and had it not been for her tear-stained face, Daisy would have questioned whether she had even seen the woman upset at all.

"I'll just go and freshen up," Daisy said, tipping the cat from her lap and ignoring his yowls of indignant displeasure.

A flash of black wings was all Daisy had seen of the elusive and very vocal 'Archie', disappearing through the kitchen and into the old boot room at the back of the property, and she did wonder at the menagerie she was expected to share her new home with. Nora and Arthur she had been prepared for, despite valuing her own space very highly – pets, not so much.

"That's new," Nora observed when they were both sitting back at the kitchen table, an old ceramic teapot filled with Yorkshire tea between them. Like everything in the vicarage, the crockery was 'vintage' in the least appealing sense of the word. None of these delicate china cups and saucers, this was wartime utility ware at its finest. To give it its due, it had served the intervening decades with only minimal chips and breakages, so Daisy assumed what it lacked in appearance it made up for in durability.

Daisy set her cup down and followed the direction of the woman's gaze, though she knew exactly where it would be levelled. Suddenly self-conscious, she wished for a moment that her walking stick was in a more conventional, fade-into-the-background colour such as black, and not the bright, multicoloured version that she had chosen the very next day after being released from her lengthy hospital stay. Having decided back then that she would not hide her disability, that she would embrace it as a part of herself, confidently and proudly, the force of Nora's unwavering stare was almost enough to cause Daisy to question her life choices.

In that moment, Daisy felt not a single drop of confidence as she quietly replied, "It is."

"Hmm," Nora said, though she had the tact to not press further for an explanation. Changing the subject completely, in fact, the woman stated, "Well, all those feet and that big hulking ambulance will have trampled my flower beds to death I imagine, not that you'd care after that stunt when you pulled up my tulips to make a daisy chain."

I was eight! Daisy exclaimed internally, though to the old lady opposite, she simply smiled and nodded, an expression she had perfected since joining the Church of England. Bea, though, Bea would have a good giggle that the infamous crime had been regurgitated so soon after their reacquaintance, tipping even a fatal accident off the top spot for topics of conversation.

Swallowing down her indignation at being made to feel like a child again, Daisy reminded herself of her vocation and took a steadying breath, "Tell me what happened today, Nora… with Arthur."

The woman's eyes pinched into thin slits and she made a show of shooing the large tom cat off the chair next to her where he had chosen to resume his snooze after being unceremoniously dumped off Daisy's knee. She refilled their cups, added more milk, tut-tutted when Daisy added another sugar lump to her own tea and finally, in a tone of complete defeat said, "It was all my fault, Vicar."

6. AN EARLY MORNING FLIGHT TO MAJORCA

Unsure whether this was some sort of confession, Daisy braced herself for the worse.

"Your fault?" She left the question deliberately open-ended, not wanting to lead the answer. Despite appearing outwardly in control, however, inside Daisy's stomach churned and she worried for a moment that she might return to the panicked state of earlier. Her mind wanted to wander to what the forensics team would be doing outside, what the detective might have found, and whether she would shortly hear the hard rap of the knocker as they came to the front door with questions to which Daisy had no answers. Past and present situations were beginning to merge in her mind, so that Daisy had to force herself to

remain calm and rational. Since her ordination, Daisy
had not questioned her calling to serve a higher
purpose. Now, though, now she was catapulted back
to those early days of questioning her new vocation –
was she really cut out for this? To minister to others in
times of crisis when it often felt like her own head was
about to explode?

The large kitchen window, still sporting the same
greyed net half-curtain that Daisy remembered from
her youth, looked out over a small, grassed garden, its
borders teeming with flowers in this summer month.
Serving both as a beautiful adornment, and also the
more important purpose of forming a partition
between the personal space of the vicarage and the
graveyard beyond, Daisy tried to remember the names
of each of the different floral varieties as she waited for
Nora to speak again. Given that her grandmother had
been a florist, and Daisy herself had spent long hours
in that shop, she had once been proficient at naming
most common varieties. Now, though, Daisy struggled
with even the exact type of hydrangea which grew just
beyond the window.

Whilst her musings helped to settle her nerves, Daisy's
lack of attention to the woman opposite her did little to
encourage an explanation. Forcing herself to focus,
Daisy tried again, "Nora, what happened to Arthur?"

"He had become quite contrary, you know, in his old age," Nora began, the deep wrinkles around the woman's eyes seeming to swallow them up completely in her displeasure, "always jaunting about the village on his little 'missions.'"

"What kind of missions?"

"Well, he had a bit of a thing… a dalliance going with Robert Briggs' sister, Lizzie, before her tragic accident a few months' back. The two of them were inseparable, gallivanting around, walking the moors, visiting the libraries here and in Whitby. Not that her brother approved, of course, Arthur would never be good enough for that man's family. Even though the woman was in her fifties and surely old enough to make her own choices. Anyway, they always had some new thing to dig up about the history of the town, or some animal in need that they needed to find a home for and Arthur would chatter on for hours if I let him. He was inconsolable after she passed."

"That's awful, Nora, you mean the Briggs family up at Bayview Farm?" Flashes of a certain brown-eyed boy from her youth flitted through Daisy's mind, and she tried to mentally shove them back in the box they had been kept in for the past fifteen years.

"Aye, 'cept they like it to be known as 'Bayview Estate'

36

now, all grand like. Timid as a mouse that woman was, but she seemed to come out of her shell with Arthur. Not that I approved of him gadding about like a teenager at his age, making his courting public, you understand."

Daisy didn't understand, no, but she made no comment on that, instead wondering, "Do you mind me asking what happened to her?"

"Fell off a cliff." It was said so bluntly and without emotion, that Daisy wondered for a second if she'd heard correctly.

"Off a cliff?"

"Aye. Like I said, tragic."

"So, ah, and forgive me again for asking, but do you think Arthur might have..?"

"Done himself in? Heartbroken like? Pah! No, he was made of harder stuff than that, he can't've lived with me for the past thirty years without getting a stronger constitution than that. No, it must've been a tragic accident."

"But what was he even doing on the church roof in the first place?"

Nora looked away towards the window, her expression washed with guilt, "Well, he loved going up there, fixing the tiles, watching the view – his happy place you could call it – up there, or up those narrow stairs in the church tower to the spire. But I must admit, today I'd put it on his list of jobs just to get him out from underfoot, while I got the place ship shape you understand. I never thought he'd... I mean, he'd never even had a wobble up there before."

"Well, you can't blame yourself," Daisy replied softly, though her head buzzed with more questions than she had answers.

When Daisy retreated to her new room shortly after that conversation, she found the space much busier than she'd anticipated. Certainly not the calming ecclesiastical retreat she had been hoping for.

"Aye," Nora nodded as she showed Daisy into the large bedroom at the opposite end of the single downstairs corridor, past the sitting room. The housekeeper herself had one of the tiny bedrooms upstairs in what was once the attic space, as did the recently deceased Arthur, though Daisy had no idea how the woman managed the stairs at her age.

"Aye, I know what you're thinking, but the last vicar left in such a hurry, and I didn't know what to do with his stuff, so..." She shrugged her shoulders, eying the electronic exercise bike and treadmill in the corner suspiciously. Daisy, too, had clocked the same machines, and couldn't help the look of distaste which she cast upon them.

Since her accident, Daisy's level of activity had been limited to church services, visiting parishioners in their homes, and the occasional light walk. Anything that could be called 'exercise' was firmly off her radar. As a result, her body that had already been well into the realm of 'curvaceous' was now more decidedly in the 'rotund' category. Not that Daisy much cared, though she made a mental note to remove the full-length Victorian mirror that stood in the opposite corner, next to an Edwardian handbasin that had definitely seen better days.

"I don't think I did hear why the previous incumbent left so suddenly?" Daisy asked, as she picked up a mug in the shape of a man's naked torso from the shelf next to the bed.

"Aye, I can understand why the Bishop wasn't keen to share the details," Nora said, her old eyes suddenly bright as if she were about to share a tasty bit of gossip, "let's just say your predecessor took off suddenly on an early morning flight to Majorca."

Daisy saw nothing so shocking in this, other than the man clearly hadn't signalled his intentions to the powers that be, until Nora added, "Coincidentally on the very same plane as the curate."

"Oh," it suddenly became clear to Daisy why the parish was also without its curatic help, another question she had not received an answer to before her journey here. She shook herself slightly as that piece of information sunk in, and then rallied, "Well, I won't be needing this exercise equipment, nor any of these protein shakes, dumbbells or, well, any of it in fact. Let's see if we can sell it for a contribution to church funds."

As Daisy turned to the huge, high, king sized bed – a rarity in ecumenical lodgings – she realised that at some point during the brief conversation a certain large, red, furry ball had snuck in and made himself comfortable on her pillows. To be sure, Jacob was the roundest, grumpiest cat that Daisy had ever come across, having clearly perfected the level of disdain that other felines can only aspire to! He regarded her now with a clear look of displeasure, ironically as if Daisy were something the cat had dragged in. It was clear he was used to ruling the roost here, but the new vicar was keen to nip that in the bud as quickly as possible.

"Nora, I..." But the older woman had already disappeared back along the narrow, musty corridor, leaving Daisy to deal with the feline interloper currently ensconced on her own bed, "Hmm, just while I fetch my things from the car then," Daisy whispered, receiving only a look of absolute haughty disgust in reply.

7. BURIED TREASURE

Giving the taped-off area a wide berth, Daisy was grateful to the new detective she met on her way back onto church grounds, her arms overflowing with her possessions. Often misjudging her own capabilities, Daisy had of course loaded up far too much at once, and the poor man only just managed to catch a box of books as it slipped from the vicar's grasp.

"I'm so sorry," Daisy tried to catch her breath and her cane at the same time, whilst the stranger held her elbow for support and balanced the box in his other hand.

"Not at all, I can ask one of the officers to give you a hand, if you like? We're all but done here, awful accident."

"Thank you, that would be very kind, Daisy Bloom, new vicar." Daisy couldn't offer her hand, otherwise occupied as it was, as they hurried forwards towards the vicarage, weaving through the worn headstones and then onto the surer footing of the flower-lined garden path.

"Detective Inspector Cluero, pleased to meet you," his kindly voice, with a soothing Welsh lilt, rolled over Daisy eliciting a calming effect. The complete opposite, in fact, to his colleague whom Daisy had run into a short while ago when she first arrived. But then, this man hadn't been her tormentor all through high school.

"You think it was just an accident, poor Arthur?" Daisy blurted out.

"Aye, that's what it seems for now, until the coroner gives his verdict. Just a fall, a very unfortunate one at that."

Daisy offered the man a cup of tea for his help, feeling it was the least she could do, though the prospect of sitting through another strained cuppa with Nora did not appeal. Thankfully, the man politely declined, and Daisy accepted the aid of a uniformed officer who transported her few belongings into the vicarage in less than half the time it would have taken her to do it herself.

The sea had always been Daisy's happy place. As a child she remembered coming here with Gran and playing in the waves, making sandcastles and hunting down shells and sea glass. Since Daisy's mum had become pregnant with her when she herself was only seventeen, and then had been killed in a hit and run collision three years later, Daisy really only had memories of her grandmother bringing her up. The name itself summons images of an older woman, greying on top and with a wealth of experience to live from. In reality, however, Daisy's grandma had been given that title when she herself was only in her very early forties, meaning that people often assumed that she was Daisy's biological mother. Daisy remembered doing nothing to dissuade them, happy to fit in when she could.

Despite having never returned after Gran's murder, Daisy had been kept up to date with the goings on in Lillymouth from Bea and had occasionally done her own online searches to see which places in the town remained the same. It was one of these that led her to

the beachfront gallery and café now. The worn wooden
sign out front confirming that it was still known as
'The Boatyard.'

"Blummin' heck! Daisy Bloom is that you?" The man
behind the counter, currently wiping his hands on his
apron before spreading his arms wide and hurrying
out to greet her was exactly as she remembered. A little
broader perhaps, greyer definitely, his beard all salt
and no pepper now, 'Uncle' Joseph Pierce was the
closest Daisy had ever had to a father figure. "Come
here, lass, come here!"

Daisy found herself enveloped in a huge bear hug –
despite the fact he must be in his mid-seventies by
now, the fisherman's strength clearly hadn't begun to
wane. It had been Gran whom the man had initially
come round to visit, all those years ago, Gran who had
refused his proposals of marriage and requests that she
and Daisy come to live with him here, down by the
water's edge, but it had been Daisy for whom he had
been a rock when the woman they both loved was
taken from them.

Daisy felt her eyes began to leak as she took in the
familiar smell of him, of salty brine mixed with freshly
brewed coffee. The feel of his coarse wool jumper
beneath her cheek brought back so many memories

that Daisy was almost reluctant to move when, at length, Joe pulled back to get a better look at her.

"Always bringing the sunshine, just as I remember," the man whispered, still holding Daisy by the shoulders. He had always called her his Viking warrior princess, as they sailed in his boat looking for pirates and across the small channel of the bay to Smugglers' Isle in search of buried treasure. Joe always left a few crates of goodness-knows-what on the island for the pirates, which he told Daisy was only polite – and they left him brown paper envelopes tied with string in return. Gran had always come too, and Daisy recalled some trips that even took them as far as France, with Joe saying he was mixing business and pleasure as the fishing boat was packed with alcohol and cigarettes for their return journey.

With her natural blonde hair in its habitual plait, her blue eyes bright from tears, Daisy supposed she did still fit that moniker to some degree. Though who she would be battling with a dodgy left side and a blunt walking stick she wasn't sure, despite the self defence training she had undertaken after recovering from her assault.

"Hush now!" Daisy scolded, embarrassed from the compliment. They had a lot to catch up on, to be sure, but in a way it felt like the missed years just fell away with the reconnection.

When they were settled on a shabby chic wooden table with a cafetière of his finest blend, the happy shouts of children on the beach blowing through the open windows, Joseph led with the question Daisy had dreaded. Not a mention of her new dog collar, nor her obvious walking aid. No. The one question that had haunted her for over a decade.

"Why did you run, lass? I would've protected you from the blasted rumours, from the lot of them. The police had not a scrap of evidence on you that wasn't circumstantial, they couldn't take you back in without finding something new."

"I know, Uncle Joe, I know, but I'd just turned eighteen, just come into my rights as the main beneficiary of Gran's will, we'd been having… words, and then just like that she was killed. The police blamed me and would've arrested me if they'd had enough proof, our neighbours turned on me, you were the only one, you and Robbie… anyway, I'm sorry, I just had to go." For a moment, Daisy was back to being that scared teenager, the one who had spent hours in interrogation rooms, who was done with this small town and all of the small-mindedness it represented,

"I'm sorry I just left, though, without saying goodbye."

"I don't need your apologies, lass, I'm just happy to see you back. I did look for you, you know, it was just my own grief was a black cloud that... anyway, you are staying aren't you?"

"If the Bishop has his say, then yes. Besides, I thought it might be about time I found some justice for Gran."

"Now Daisy, don't you be going investigating by yerself. I've done my own searching, over the years, and always came up blank. I mean, there's that high and mighty Robert Briggs, I wouldn't put anything past him. But he's a slippery devil – you can never lay anything directly at his door. Then there's that weird bloke who was so keen to snap up the florist's shop, I made sure Percy Glendinning at the bank got the money from the sale to your account though."

"I know, I know, thank you. Yes, I've met him, the florist, strange, sleazy man."

"He hasn't done anything improper? You just tell me if..."

"No, no, just made some lecherous comments that's all. Yes, I got the money from the sale into my bank account, thank you. But I must admit I wanted none of it. Sense must've prevailed even through my grief, however, because I used it to train as a victim liaison officer and then to open a refuge for victims of domestic violence, so Gran's hard work went towards something good, at least."

"You always were one to stand up for others, Daisy. Your Gran would be so proud of you."

Daisy tried ineffectually to swallow down the ball of emotion that had become lodged in her throat, eventually taking a large gulp of her coffee. Seeing her distress, Joe filled the silence with chat about the townsfolk and about his own paintings until some colour had returned to the vicar's cheeks.

"Have you caught up with anyone yet?"

"Only Bea… and Nora Clumping. Actually, I came straight down here after I'd dumped my stuff in the vicarage. Needed the air. Did you hear about Arthur?"

"Arthur? No. It's been awful seeing him these past couple of months grieving Lizzie Briggs. This was their favourite meeting spot, you know. They even bought some of my artwork to save for when they wed next year, not that they'd told anyone else about that I don't think."

"That is sad, Uncle Joe, even more so because Arthur himself passed this morning."

"No! I knew the man was devastated by the loss, but I didn't realise he was that desperate…"

"No, I mean, that was my first question too, but no, it was apparently just a tragic accident. He fell while sorting out some tiles on the church roof, bless him."

"He always was a hard worker, and Nora gave him no credit for everything he did round there for free. The church didn't pay him either." His eyes flicked to Daisy's dog collar, though the old seafarer still didn't ask the question.

Daisy could tell that the man's opinions on the Church of England hadn't softened over the years, and she didn't want to get into a discussion on religion when they had just become reacquainted, so joked instead, "I'm guessing I won't see you at the service on Sunday then?"

"Definitely not, but you're welcome round here for a hot dinner after, if you like?" Joe gestured to his home which consisted of a few rooms attached at the side of the café building, "I'm guessing you have a few tales to tell?" He nodded at Daisy's stick, propped against the side of the table, but his kind eyes shone with their usual warmth which soothed Daisy's habitual bristles at any reference to her altered abilities.

"I would love to accept, but I fear I may be expected back at the vicarage for my first Sunday roast since taking up the post. Even if just to keep Nora company."

"That old battle-axe wouldn't care either way, but it's up to you, the invitation's there."

"Thank you. And we will have a proper catch-up soon, I promise."

Daisy cast a final glance around the place as she put on her light jacket to leave. The coffee shop hadn't changed much – different watercolour pictures adorned the walls, but all still had a coastal theme. The rustic, white painted wood of the tables and chairs was the same, as was the faded bunting that hung at the windows. The main thing this old café had going for it was the uninhibited views of the North sea and the miles of beach.

A view that would never go out of date.

8. YOU CAN SAVE YOUR PLEASANTRIES, VICAR

Daisy had been up late writing the first sermon that she was to deliver in her new parish. The first parish that was truly hers, in fact, since her previous role had been as curate and not the main incumbent. She wanted something that was pithy and memorable, with the right balance of scripture and inspiration. As it was, all she had been able to come up with were tried and tested texts that she felt did nothing to light a fire in the congregation. Nothing that would be memorable.

Perhaps that's it, Daisy thought as she grumpily dressed in her freezing cold room, *perhaps I'm worried about making any impact on these people who used to be my neighbours, wanting to make them see me in a new light. The same ones who turned on me when Gran died. Maybe I'm putting too much weight on their opinions?* Not for the first time, Daisy wished she had been given a post somewhere brand new, without the historical ties of her childhood in Lillymouth.

Her sour mood, caused from being over tired and underprepared, had been heightened by the sound of church bells ringing throughout the cottage at, what Daisy discovered to be, the ridiculous hour of six in the morning. Dragging herself from her bed and peering out from under the net curtain at her window, Daisy had seen no movement from the church or belfry. Muttering to herself, she had opened her door to go and ask Nora whether this was normal, when Daisy had been confronted by a black bird, perched on the curtain rail in the hallway. The shrill sound coming from its yellow beak – the perfect impersonation of church bells – halted abruptly the moment the creature locked eyes with Daisy, and there they both froze in silent inspection of the other.

"What even are you?" Daisy muttered eventually, jumping in shock as Nora appeared silently at the bottom of the narrow staircase, looking the part of a ghost in her white nightdress.

"He's a mynah bird, sent by the devil to distract me to madness," Nora said solemnly.

Daisy dragged her gaze from the woman back to the bird, who had been thankfully quiet in the few days since her arrival. So much so, in fact, that Daisy had almost forgotten the creature's existence. Clearly he had simply been biding his time.

"Why on earth did the curate want this bird for a pet?" Daisy asked, to which the feathered impressionist started up with "Not today, thank you!" and after five rounds of the chant, disappeared in the direction of the kitchen.

"Well, we're up now, best make a start on the day," Nora had said, following after the black shadow to put the kettle on.

Daisy had been keen to disagree, and to get another hour or so of sleep, but she hadn't mastered the ability to say no to her housekeeper yet, so here she was, getting dressed at dawn in a room with no radiator. *What had her predecessor done to keep warm?* She wondered, before quickly locking down the mental image which followed.

A quick prayer in the vestry before the service had given Daisy enough confirmation to tackle the theme of acceptance and tolerance, which had come to her as she sat in the vicarage kitchen at seven that morning. Two things that, so the bishop had told her, were still sorely lacking in the small town.

"Go big or go home," Daisy whispered to herself, just as a familiar face poked her head around the door.

"Bea, thank goodness, please tell me there's only you and a handful of others out there."

"Ah, no, not quite, it seems the return of Lillymouth's prodigal daughter has attracted quite a crowd."

"Fabulous. That's just fabulous," Daisy said, adjusting her cassock self-consciously, and then to the heavens she exclaimed, "You'd better know what You're doing, because I certainly don't!"

If her best friend thought it odd that Daisy was seemingly communicating directly with God she said nothing, simply gave the vicar a quick hug and disappeared the way she had come.

"... So I said, we could make a bunch of blooms! Get it?" The booming tones of Gerald Bunch met Daisy as she walked into the main chapel of the church. The man possessed such a loud confidence, that everyone around was forced to bathe in it. Thankfully, he was drowned out then by the sounds of the church organ starting up, somewhat belatedly. The woman playing the instrument was tiny, almost no bigger than a child, and Daisy wondered how her feet even reached the pedals. The notes of 'All Things Bright and Beautiful' were more clanking than smooth, but the tune was at least recognisable and Daisy took a deep breath before walking slowly to the pulpit. The smell of lilies and furniture polish which permeated the space was a familiar comfort, though it could not detract from the feeling of so many eyes upon her, many of them no doubt hostile.

Daisy forced herself to look up as she took her position at the front, scanning the crowd for a brief second. Relieved, her eyes locked onto those of a woman she would always recognise – Sylvia Carmichael, her grandmother's erstwhile best friend. Remarkably still blonde and red-lipped despite the fact she must be nearing seventy, the kindly woman smiled widely at Daisy, even going so far as to give her a quick wave of her hand, and Daisy felt the butterflies in her stomach begin to slow. The sight of her goddaughter, tiny Daisy Mae, on the front row helped to further alleviate her nerves, so that Daisy felt she at least had the strength to begin.

She announced the first hymn, and put all her trust in
He who had brought her to this exact moment in this
specific place, only slightly perturbed when the
familiar tune of 'All Things Bright and Beautiful' began
to ring out again.

This was the part that Daisy had been dreading the
most – greeting her parishioners as they exited the
building. She tried to discreetly wipe her sweating
palms on her robes whilst nodding and smiling as
families introduced their small children, whose names
Daisy had no hope of remembering. She was acting so
much on autopilot that the next person in the queue
took her unawares, and Daisy had no time to steel
herself.

"Miss Bloom," Robert Briggs offered his hand,
towering over Daisy with a look that could only be
described as thunderous.

"It's Reverend Bloom now, Dad," the man beside him
corrected, causing Daisy to look up and straight into
the eyes of the only boy she had ever loved – if teenage
lust and emotional dependency could be considered
love, she supposed. He had been handsome as a youth,

so the young Daisy had thought anyway, but the man before her now could be described as nothing short of beautiful, all chiselled cheeks and dark, floppy hair with the short stubble that was apparently so fashionable nowadays. Not that it affected Daisy in any way, that ship had long since sailed.

"Robbie, it's good to see you," Daisy said, yanking her hand back from the rough grasp of the man's father.

"And you," he replied, giving Daisy the same lingering, scalding look that would have once made her melt, "I hope we can catch up properly soon."

Before Daisy could reply, however, Briggs Senior interrupted them, "Aye well, that's not likely, you moved back to help me with the estate remember. You just got rid of that awful bit of skirt you married, you don't need another getting her claws in. And as for you, Vicar, you must really believe in miracles if you think you could ever have a fresh start here."

"Well, I…" Daisy began, incredulous at the man's rudeness, but he had already stalked off. Instead, to his son, she said, "I see he hasn't changed."

"No, if anything he's worse now that we're expanding the place," he looked like he was about to say more, save for the loud tut from the woman behind him in the queue, "anyway, I'll be in touch."

Daisy wasn't sure she wanted him to be, but the man was already rushing after his father, and there would've been no way to decline his interest in a catch-up without sounding rude. Besides, Daisy figured she could use all the allies she could get in this town, the notion reinforced as she came face to face with Violet Glendinning, chair of the parish council, wife of the local bank manager, and all round busybody.

"Mrs. Glendinning," Daisy began, only to be halted mid-sentence by the woman herself.

"You can save your pleasantries, Vicar, we both know you won't last long enough here to necessitate us getting along," and with that the woman left Daisy open-mouthed, her tall, willowy frame belying the rod of steel that she clearly had shoved up her a... Daisy took a deep breath and tried to have more godly thoughts.

9. ALL THINGS BRIGHT AND BEAUTIFUL

It was a weary vicar who came into the vicarage kitchen an hour later to find the housekeeper feeding the cat double cream from a bowl on the kitchen table of all places. Daisy didn't have the strength to protest as the victorious creature eyed her sidewise whilst lapping greedily. It was very clear who enabled his feeling of lordship over them, but Daisy didn't want to get into an argument with Nora, not when they still had to sit together and eat the roast dinner which the older woman had prepared.

"So, ah, does the organist know any other hymns?" Daisy asked, when they had eaten in uncomfortable silence for the first five minutes.

"What? Mildred Spratt? No, only that one. She tries, bless her, but however hopeful they start out, the songs always sound like 'All Things Bright and Beautiful.' The congregation are used to just singing any words to that tune now." Nora said it so matter-of-factly, as if that was how it was done and there was no chance of ever changing it – a sentiment shared by many of the locals on many issues, Daisy feared – that she offered no space for debate on the subject.

Of course Daisy had suggestions – quite a few of them, in fact – but for now she kept them to herself, respectful of the fact that Nora was clearly and understandably grieving. At least there had been no further appearances from the police, for which Daisy was very grateful.

Daisy washed and dried the dishes, shooing Nora away into the sitting room with a pot of tea in the hope of enjoying some peace and quiet. The solid, upright wingback chairs in that room suited the housekeeper, but Daisy didn't plan on spending much time in there given that the space was hardly conducive to relaxation. An old, dark wood Edwardian china cabinet and side tables, which had been polished to within an inch of their lives over the years, added to the austere gloom of the sitting room, meaning the vicar much preferred the brighter – if not any more modern – kitchen.

Her peace was short-lived, however, when a shrill barking sound came from the adjoining boot room. Jacob moved faster than Daisy had hitherto assumed the fat cat could, charging straight towards the noise with a howl of righteous indignation that a cursed canine had been allowed into his space. Daisy followed hot on his paws, only to see the cat skid to a halt in front of her when met only by the mynah bird, its piercing eyes almost laughing at them from his perch on top of the washing machine.

"Archie!" Daisy exclaimed, though she was drowned out by the sound of Jacob clawing at the old machine, desperate to get his hefty weight off the floor and on top of the metal from where the bird mocked him. Judging by the deep gouges already present where he clawed, this was not the first time this scene had played out, and Daisy felt her annoyance grow. The mynah bird, claiming victory, took off with a swoop over their heads and out through the kitchen, leaving the cat panting and furious.

"Grr!" Daisy growled in a decidedly un-ecumenical fashion, stomping back the way she had come and deciding that a walk in the fresh air would be good for her soul.

The sun on her face and the sea breeze at her back brought Daisy back to a state of almost-equilibrium. She pondered the morning's church service as she walked down Cobble Wynd, careful not to lose her footing on the ancient stones. Being a Sunday, most of the shops were closed, though those that sold souvenirs, ice creams or anything that could be attractive to the summer tourists in the town were open in this season. It had always been Bea's aunt's prerogative to make hay while the sun shone, so she opened the bookshop with its quaint tearoom every day of the week in the summer months. Daisy remembered helping Bea behind the counter there when they were younger and then running up the Wynd to help her Gran with the flower deliveries.

So today, as she reached the bottom corner of the cobbled street, Daisy hoped that Bea had kept up that tradition. She had drunk enough of Nora's weak tea in the past few days to make even the thought of a cappuccino too much to resist. As Daisy tried the door and found it unlocked, she said a quick prayer of thanks heavenward, that at least the Good Lord hadn't sent her to a place bereft of caffeine.

It was Bea's husband, Andrew, who stood behind the

long wooden counter serving a little girl who was buying a book and a postcard of the town, and Daisy waited patiently until he was free.

"Daisy, I haven't had a chance to say a proper hello," Andrew said, coming around the counter to hug Daisy, who tapped him awkwardly on the back.

"Yes, Bea tells me your joinery business is on the up and up, that's fantastic."

"Aye, well, if Briggs gets the go ahead for his plans up at the estate then I'll have a lot of guaranteed work coming, coffee?" At her nod he led Daisy to the tea nook at the back, which was empty of customers.

"That's great news. Please don't turn the machine on for me," Daisy said politely, though inside she hoped the opposite.

"Don't be silly, it's all set up and ready to go in case of any takers. Not that we get many on Sundays unless the weather's bad, mostly they stay down at the beach and in the park. Shall I tell Bea you're here? She's just upstairs nursing Daisy Mae."

"No, no don't disturb them," Daisy replied, looking forward to sitting in peace with her coffee. There would be plenty of time for baby snuggles and catch-ups now that she was back in the town permanently.

The sound of the door chime called Andrew back
down to that end of the shop as soon as he had made
her drink, leaving Daisy in quiet contemplation. The
delicious aroma of the roasted coffee beans mixed with
the almost musty smell of old leather and new books
was a heady combination for Daisy, and a scent which
tripped her mind straight back to her youth. Often,
Bea's mum Morag would bring the two girls here to
visit her sister, Bea's aunt, letting them choose a book
each before taking them down to the beach to play in
the sand. She had never treated Daisy any differently
to her own daughter, and had at times seemed like a
second mum. Whilst Bea's father had been grumpy
and aloof, never keen for Daisy to hang around with
Bea in their home, his wife had bestowed a kindness on
Daisy that she would never forget.

Daisy made a mental note to ask Bea how her parents
were doing just as a shadowed figure loomed ahead of
her, blocking the sunlight from the front window and
doorway.

"Daisy! It must be my lucky day," Robbie stepped
forward, raised a questioning eyebrow at the seat next
to her, and then sat down when Daisy gave him the go
ahead.

Thankful that at least he wasn't Gerald Bunch, Daisy stifled her sigh and affixed her people-facing façade back in place.

"It's lovely to see you again, Robbie," Daisy said, silently finding it funny how even the clergy couldn't get away from telling white lies.

"It's a long time since anyone's called me that, I've been Rob since… well since you left actually. It's good to hear you say my old nickname again, Dee-Dee."

Hearing the old pet term nearly caused Daisy to shoot straight out of her seat, so uncomfortable did it make her feel. Rob carried on oblivious to her discomfort, however, and she made a note to not refer to the man as Robbie ever again. When she forced herself to tune back in to what he was saying, Daisy wished she hadn't had to.

"… I mean, sorry to lead with this after so long apart, but you must've known I would've come with you. At the time I even asked my dad if you could stay with us, you can imagine how hard that was for me and, well, you know what an old curmudgeon he was – and he's even worse now – but even after his refusal all was not lost, I would have left with you, if you hadn't just disappeared. You broke my hear…"

"Can I get you anything?" Andrew interrupted at that very opportune moment and Daisy hoped her sigh of relief wasn't audible to both men. Grateful, she smiled at her friend's husband as he took Rob's order and tried to down her own coffee as fast as she could without burning her throat.

"Thank you for supporting me, back then," Daisy said, by way of closing that topic of conversation.

As Rob jumped in with, "Of course I supported you, I loved yo…" Daisy did some interrupting of her own and changed the subject to something much drier and hopefully less emotional.

"So, I hear your dad is planning to expand? It seems that a lot has happened up at what used to be Briggs' Farm. Oh, I'm so sorry to hear about your Aunt Lizzie, she was always a lovely woman." Daisy kicked herself for not leading with that. She needed to find 'vicar Daisy' again, before 'Lillymouth reject Daisy' said anything inflammatory.

"She was, I hadn't long returned to the town when we lost her. She'd always been fiercely independent, but walking along the cliff path when strong winds were forecast, well… Dad was devastated, of course, she being his only relative left apart from me, but handled it stoically in his usual outwardly indifferent way."

Daisy could well imagine, "So, you're just back temporarily?" She could hope, at least.

"Ah, actually no, just went through a messy divorce, very expensive, and Dad needs me to project manage the works so…"

"It sounds like a big undertaking?" Daisy took her last gulp and made a show of setting down her mug and picking up her cheesecloth backpack.

"Yes, it should be, converting outbuildings to three-storey luxury apartments and building spa facilities, a restaurant and gym. Plus turning a field into a windfarm to supply all the energy for that… well, I won't bother you with the details, it's dad's baby not mine. And you know how he doesn't do things by halves when he gets his mind fixed on something. There's no backing down or deviating from the plan till it's complete. Not exactly what I signed up for when I came back, the place isn't what it used to be… well, it wasn't until you came back…"

Daisy smiled and nodded, whilst thinking all the while what an awful eyesore that would make on the skyline outside the town and deliberately ignoring the man's references to their more personal relationship that, in her opinion, was very much dead and buried, "Well, I'd best get going."

"I'll walk you back up to the vicarage, I'm guessing Nora will be spending the late afternoon out having tea with her cronies as she does every week."

"No! No, ah, I like to pray – in, um, solitude on Sunday afternoons," another white lie wouldn't hurt, she was sure, "I'm heading for a walk down one of the piers I think."

Daisy pretended she hadn't noticed either the hurt look in the man's eyes or the way his gaze lingered a fraction too long on her chest. She felt herself blush as she hurriedly said her goodbyes and rushed out into the welcome fresh air, her cane tapping a staccato beat as she made a beeline for the promenade.

10. DÉJÀ-VU

It was a very bad-tempered vicar who returned to the vicarage much later that afternoon, in need of painkillers, alcohol and a deep bath, not necessarily in that order. That she was met on the path outside by a very loud mynah bird making siren noises should have alerted Daisy to the fact that something was wrong. So tired was she, however, that even the front door standing slightly ajar didn't set her own alarm bells ringing the way it should have. The Daisy of former years would've engaged hairs-standing-on-end, heart thumping, adrenaline fuelled, full defensive mode by now. Goodness knows she'd had enough experiences in her past role where Daisy had had to rely on the gut feeling that told her something was 'off' about a person or a place. Here, though, in good old Lillymouth, even when she had literal siren sounds ringing in her ears, Daisy seemed to have flicked an internal switch to turn her into a bumbling, trusting idiot.

As a result, the vicar almost tripped over the body of Nora Clumping which lay at the foot of the stairs, just to the left of the large, antique coat stand.

Daisy stopped short, her body lurching forwards using the tip of her cane as a pivot, before righting herself and swallowing down the bile which rose swiftly to the back of her throat. From the ungodly angle that Nora's head sat in relation to her neck and shoulders, Daisy was pretty sure the cause of death was a fall down the stairs. The way her legs were twisted beneath her and her arms bent to what should be an impossible degree all contributed to give the old woman an almost grotesque outline. In her head, Daisy saw it as it would look drawn in the chalk of a forensic demarcation line, detaching herself from the fact that she knew the poor woman who lay there.

Forcing herself to move closer and to bend down, Daisy checked for a pulse, just in case, though she wasn't surprised to find none. Jacob had curled himself into the space between his mistress's legs and was eying Daisy warily, his body that normally rolled and jiggled now tense and rigid under his thick ginger fur.

Daisy stood again, her every movement feeling sluggish and as if she was walking through thick treacle. It was like she was shutting down, numbing herself lest the threatening panic take hold and she lose all control.

"Psst, Psss," Daisy made ineffectual noises to try to get the cat to move away before swiftly giving up and hurrying along the corridor to her own room. Searching through the larger of the two boxes which she had yet to unpack, Daisy found the bottle of cask strength Bunnahabhain that had been an ordination gift. Despite her shaking hands, the cork released with a satisfying pop and Daisy inhaled the whisky fumes as if they were smelling salts. Although tempted to forego a glass altogether, she quickly grabbed the empty water beaker from her tiny handbasin and poured a generous glug of the amber liquid. One swig, then a second straight after to avoid the coughing fit that would surely lead to vomiting over what she had come upon, and Daisy focused on the burning feeling travelling down her throat and chest.

She set the empty cup beside the bottle and did a slow breathing exercise for ten seconds before calmly getting her mobile phone from her bag and dialling 999. The whole feeling that this was some cruel and complicated form of déjà-vu settled on Daisy as she spoke to the police call handler, not even recognising her own voice and surprised that her body wasn't shaking like a leaf as she perched on the end of her bed. They asked questions and she answered on autopilot, only brought back to the room and out of her own head fully when she felt a heavy weight land on her lap. Daisy stroked the soft fur and accepted the forehead rubs against her palm of the cat who had come to share in her pain, and was even grateful for them. The Lord knew, she could do with a friend right about now.

"So, you came in, you saw the deceased and you went to your room, down the corridor there? You did not go upstairs?" Detective Matlock posed the question that Daisy had already answered three times since the full force of the local police had descended on the quiet vicarage.

"Exactly. First, I was in no state to investigate further. Second, Nora was blocking the stairs, I would've had to step over her," Daisy felt her lower lip tremble and turned her head away.

"And you called the police and not an ambulance? Were you inebriated when you returned vicar? I can certainly smell alcohol on you now. Did you perhaps get into an argument with your housekeeper and…"

"No! Nora was lying there when I came in, stone cold sober. I checked her and found no pulse, knew the paramedics could've done nothing to save her," Daisy surprised herself with the coherency of her argument, "Besides, don't you think it too much of a coincidence that she and Arthur both died within a week of each other? Both deaths can't be accidental, surely?"

"We'll see. You'll need to come to the station to give a formal statement tomorrow and find somewhere else to stay tonight." There was no compassion in the woman's tone, not that Daisy expected there to be. Michelle Matlock's severe demeanour matched her image – her dark hair scraped back and greased down into a submissive bun at the back of her head. *Even her hair daren't move out of place,* Daisy thought.

Daisy wasn't sure she could face the interview room at the small local police station, it having become a scarier, more oppressive place in her memories than it had ever probably been in real life. But she had been only eighteen, out of her mind with grief and anger, and everything she could remember from that time had been augmented in her head over the years.

Daisy sat at the kitchen table when the detective left the room, unable to will her body to move. The hours had passed quickly in the flurry of activity and despite the summer month it was getting dark outside. She knew she needed to make arrangements for the night, but her overwhelmed brain was struggling to settle on the best option. There was Bea of course, but the guestroom in her small flat over the bookshop had likely been turned into a nursery. Uncle Joe would take her in in a heartbeat, she knew, but that would mean driving down to the seafront and then walking along to the café, something Daisy wasn't sure she could manage right now.

The large furry lump of the cat who had been her shadow these past few hours curled around her ankles, his presence a surprising reassurance as Daisy began to pray for guidance. Whether by divine providence or the universe finally giving her a break, she heard a familiar voice then, arguing with Matlock. Despite the detective's protests, the door to the kitchen burst open and Sylvia appeared, her peroxide hair in curlers and her face greasy with night cream.

"I heard the sirens, lass, and I saw the gossip on social media as to what might be happening, so I came to give you some support."

Daisy could only imagine what the internet had given to a town already so prone to indulging in gossip –

whether it was fact based or not – but didn't have the headspace to think about that now.

"Thank you, Sylvia, I could actually do with a friend."

"Of course petal, I'll put a pot of tea on to brew."

"Actually, could we have that at your house? I'm sorry to ask, I just seem to find myself with nowhere to stay for the night…"

"Why yes, you should've got a message to me!" The older woman had to help Daisy to her feet, something which would normally bring embarrassment and a misplaced sense of shame, but Daisy was numb to that for now.

"What about Jacob and Archie?"

"Archie?" Sylvia seemed confused.

"The mynah bird – don't ask – will they be okay?"

"I should think so, they'll have food and water already out for them in the boot room I suspect. I can check before we leave."

Satisfied that that responsibility had been taken from her, if just for the evening, Daisy pushed any guilt about the creatures out of her mind and allowed herself to be guided down to her bedroom to pack a small bag, the scornful eyes of Michelle Matlock burning into her back as she went.

11. AN ULTERIOR MOTIVE

"So, you don't work at the library anymore?" Daisy sipped her chamomile tea and tried to pretend that she wasn't under the beady-eyed assessment of Sylvia's extremely large, white house rabbit, Malone.

What is it with people and pets? Daisy wondered to herself, not for the first time that week. Though she was softening towards Jacob...

"No lass, the council retired me a few years back. My Ron and I had grand ideas of retiring to a villa in Spain or cruising the Med in the winter months, then he passed away suddenly and, well, here I still am. We never had the finances to do it anyway, just pipe dreams really. I do some volunteering in the town hall to fill a bit of my time."

"I'm so sorry," Daisy said, "he was a lovely man."

Daisy eyed the older woman thoughtfully.

"What is it lass? Spit it out."

"It's just, everyone else has asked me why I left without telling them, but not you."

"No, I understood why you left, and your Gran wouldn't have wanted you to stay in a place where suspicion and whispers followed you everywhere you went. No, Bea shared with me the odd bit of news here and there and I was just happy to know you were making a life for yourself. My question would be, why did you even come back?"

"Well, that wasn't really my choice, though it is a question I have been asking in my daily prayers," Daisy shrugged her shoulders and watched as the rabbit hopped towards the sofa she was sitting on. Sylvia's home was the opposite of the vicarage, warm and cosy with soft furnishings and personal knick-knacks aplenty. When Daisy had complimented the woman on it, however, Sylvia's usual cheeriness had been replaced by a mask of sadness which she struggled to hide. Given the day she had had, though,

Daisy didn't have the mental capacity to give it any thought.

"Poor Nora, eh," Sylvia said, changing the subject, "it must've been grief that made her weak and led to her fall, bless her. I've watched enough true crime shows and cop series to know what havoc unexpected death wreaks upon the mind and body of those left behind."

"Ah, perhaps," Daisy replied ambivalently, not really wanting to think about the alternative.

Sylvia, Daisy decided at lunchtime the next day as she walked back to the vicarage from the church, was worth her weight in gold. Behind the bouffant hairdo, clouds of perfume and costume jewellery was a woman with a big heart and with a wealth of common sense. When Cluero had come with a uniformed officer early in the day to take Daisy to the station to give her statement, Sylvia had outright told the detective what an insensitive and unnecessary trip that would be, given the vicar's past and her present role as parish incumbent.

"Wouldn't it make much more sense," Sylvia had argued, "to interview the vicar in the church? For surely she would never lie in the house of God."

Daisy had kept quiet while the Welshman considered the notion, grateful for the solid warmth of Sylvia's hand in hers. At length, after speaking in hushed whispers over the phone with Matlock, whose stormy, negative response from the other end of the conversation could be clearly heard, the detective had acted of his own accord and had agreed.

The panic which Daisy had felt since waking had been calmed, not least because Sylvia had gone back to the vicarage whilst Daisy was in the church and had tidied the place as best she could around the forensics team who were still finishing their investigation, a solid, plastic police tape preventing anyone else from going upstairs. When Daisy returned, the animals had been fed, there was a lasagne in the oven, and a jar of fresh flowers from the garden sat on the kitchen table.

"You are a Godsend, Sylvia, really," Daisy gave the woman a quick, one-armed hug. She wasn't really prone to random displays of affection, but couldn't think of a better way to express her gratitude in that moment.

"Well, I ah, I may have an ulterior motive lass," Sylvia looked more than sheepish, she appeared positively sick.

"Really?" Daisy sat down heavily at the table, not

getting even a second to catch her breath before Jacob landed on her knees, all fluff and whiskers. Not comfortable with his attentions yet, though she understood the animal's grief, Daisy tried ineffectually to gently push him off. Jacob was having none of it, merely digging his claws painfully into her thighs and so forcing Daisy to give up on the attempt. This gave her a few seconds to consider Sylvia's confession, which the vicar did find rather ominous, but then she silently rebuked herself for having seen the worst in everyone and everything since her return to Lillymouth.

Petting the cat distractedly, Daisy indicated for Sylvia to take the chair opposite and waited for her to continue.

"Well, ah, do you remember when your Gran was here, I mean, that is, not long before she passed, and Briggs had decided his latest project would be to buy up as much of the town as possible?"

"How could I forget? That man made Gran's last months unbearable trying to persuade her to sell. How Gerald Bunch got the shop in the end, I've no idea."

"Aye well, Briggs bought up most of the old cottages on Broad Street, including mine. My Ron thought it was a good deal, and a couple of years later when he was made redundant, we were glad of the money in the bank."

"But Briggs let you live there?"

"Yes, it was meant to be a temporary rental contract, but it seemed his plans and sights moved elsewhere, or else someone put a stop to the department store he intended because my tenancy has been renewed every year since. Until this one. I imagine the man wants to liquidise his assets to pay for the grand plans he has up at the farm. Anyway, that means I've only got a week left…"

"… To find a new place to live," Daisy put two and two together quickly – it didn't take a genius to see what her Grandma's best friend was asking, and why she would consider the timing less than perfect.

"Exactly, lass, I've been burying my head in the sand I'm afraid, hoping for a miracle," Sylvia had her hands clasped so tightly together on the tabletop that her knuckles were white. A match to her face, which had turned very pale even under the thick foundation she wore.

Daisy took a moment to consider. On the one hand, the timing couldn't be worse – she had only just come to the parish, the previous housekeeper had literally just passed away, and there was no guarantee there would be the funds for a new one. On the other, they were both of them in need of company and security, perhaps now more than ever. Sylvia was lacking in funds and therefore in housing options, and Daisy knew she would not get through another murder investigation without friends at her side.

"I'm sorry, lass, I shouldn't have asked, I've put you in an awful position…"

"No, no, it's not that, I'm just thinking. Obviously I can't ask for the parish to fill the housekeeper role so soon."

"Of course, no, no it would be the height of insensitivity, poor woman, may she rest in peace."

"So, why don't you move in and when the time's right I'll ask about the job."

"Are you sure? Oh, thank you, Daisy, thank you, I can pay you rent money…"

"No, I won't hear of it, it will be good for me to have you here. Though I fear we may have a bumpy road ahead of us in the near future at least."

As it turned out, 'bumpy' didn't even begin to cover it.

12. A REAL ANIMAL LOVER

When Sylvia had gone back home to begin her packing, Daisy stood at the foot of the stairs, knowing she needed to go up and see if Nora's room was tidy enough for Sylvia to move in. Daisy knew that it would be, of course, spotless in fact, and she certainly didn't intend on packing up any of the old woman's effects so soon. Besides, the yellow police tape cordoning off the stairs and upper floor was still firmly in place and Daisy didn't want to risk Matlock's wrath by moving it. She simply hovered there, deep in thought, until a knocking on the front door brought her out of her musings.

"Detective Cluero, please come in," Daisy said, relieved to see it was the pleasanter of the two investigators assigned to the case.

"Thank you, Vicar, my apologies for bothering you."

"Not at all, I was just contemplating why the stairs still need to be taped off when poor Nora's body is gone and the forensics team have finished their sweep."

"Matlock told me she'd already informed you," the man moved from one foot to the other uncomfortably, setting off the first flurry of panic in Daisy's stomach.

"Informed me of what?"

"The deceased lady was likely pushed down the stairs because she interrupted an intruder. The late lodger, ah, Arthur Smith, his room had been half turned upside down, so clearly someone was looking for something."

No wonder people kept asking me if I'd been upstairs, Daisy thought, though outwardly she focused on trying to remain composed, "I can't believe it, what could someone possibly want from Arthur? Surely this points to him having been deliberately killed? And how did Michelle expect me to find out? When the burglar came back for a second try and finished me off too?" Her voice rose hysterically with each question, until Daisy caught herself and took a deep breath.

Daisy studied the man opposite more closely as he

seemed to be considering how to reply. They had moved into the sitting room but neither sat down. Daisy didn't use her walking stick in the house, so she relied on the arm of the closest wingback chair to rest on. The detective himself looked exhausted, his jawline sporting more than a few days of stubble and his hair that was just beginning to grey looking dishevelled and greasy. Daisy felt a stab of compassion for the man, wondering what his back story might be. That was one of her strengths, she had been told, seeing the bigger picture of how a person's past informed and directed their present and supporting them accordingly.

"Ah, it is looking likely, yes," Cluero answered at length, the worry lines in his forehead more pronounced as he spoke, "that his death may have been deliberate, I mean. That's why I'm here in fact, since we considered Mr. Smith's death an accident at the time, we now need to backtrack and consider the details of his fall more carefully. With that in mind, I was hoping to see the ladder he was using that day to access the church roof."

"Oh, I'm not sure where that would be," Daisy said, realising she hadn't had the time since she arrived to explore the church and its grounds fully, "would you like a cup of tea or coffee and then we can look for it?"

Where that invitation came from, the vicar didn't know, but when the detective jumped at the chance of a hot drink and a sit down she was happy to oblige.

When the kettle was boiled and Cluero had removed the tape and then given Jacob the attention that the cat deemed himself deserving of, Daisy made them a pot of tea and sat opposite her visitor at the kitchen table. Just as the man opened his mouth to speak, however, the shrill sound of a phone ringing interrupted them. Cluero reached into his pocket for his mobile, but that device was silent. Daisy knew it wasn't her own ringtone and sighed heavily as she rose to her feet again.

"Excuse me detective, that'll be Archie, I'll just pop out to the boot room and tell him to be quiet. He's very attention-seeking," Daisy caught Cluero's perplexed look as she left to quieten the bird, his all-too-regular outbursts grating on her nerves.

"Archie?" the detective asked as Daisy re-joined him at the table.

"The previous curate thought it would be funny to call him the Archbishop of York and to allow him to imitate familiar sounds, being that he's a mynah bird," Daisy replied, no trace of humour in her voice.

Cluero gave her a look full of sympathy and said, "Well, strange choice of pet, rather you than me. You must be a real animal lover."

Daisy forced a weak smile and said nothing further on the subject of her inherited menagerie. An animal lover she certainly was not.

Having the tact to see when a change of topic was required, Cluero came close to surprising Daisy with his next question, "What made you become a vicar, if you don't mind me asking? We had to do a background check, I know you'll understand as I've seen that you used to work for the force in Leeds as a victim liaison officer. Strange jump, if you don't mind me saying. Was there one case in particular that prompted the change in vocation?"

"Like a 'Road to Damascus' moment?" Daisy was not a stranger to people questioning her decision to take the cloth, she just hadn't expected this detective to make such a personal query that was unrelated to the case.

"Ah, yes, something like that," Cluero looked more uncomfortable the more he spoke, "Was it one thing in particular or the cumulative effect of everything you'd seen?"

"Well, my grandma was a church goer, but I wasn't at

all religious until I met one particular woman quite a few years ago now, who had been through... horrific things. She came into the refuge I helped run and walked her path of recovery and the case to prosecute her assailant with such grace and... it's hard to explain, there was just this sense of new-found strength and resilience about her, and when I asked about it she said a friend had led her to Jesus. I silently scoffed at that notion at first, but I still had so much baggage from my own past, and new experiences too weighing me down, that I started to go to the local church. Only a couple of Sundays a month, not a big commitment or anything."

"Did you find what you were looking for?"

"Honestly? No. It wasn't until I was assaulted myself a few years back that I had time to reflect for the first time in years. Lying in that hospital bed, I knew I had to... dig deeper," Daisy took a deep breath and a large gulp of tea. It was unlike her to share so much so easily, but as it turned out Detective Cluero was a very good listener.

"The attack led to your disability?" He said it in the matter-of-fact way of seasoned policemen that Daisy was very familiar with.

"It did," Daisy replied just as dispassionately, "I

couldn't stay in my job, I took more of a back seat at the refuge too, and I completely re-evaluated my life."

Cluero pondered that for a long moment and Daisy wondered if he would share some of his own story. She had long ago learned not to push these things, though, so when he downed his tea, stood up and suggested they look for the ladder, she wasn't at all offended.

It was not a difficult job to find the small storage room next to the vestry at the back of the church. There was no lock on the door, and judging by the thick layer of dust that covered most of its contents, it was not frequently visited. A single bulb hung from the centre of the ceiling and a little fold-out chair – dust free as it happened – sat in one corner with a dirty tea cup on the floor beside it. It was clear that Nora's duster had never discovered this place, making it the perfect hideout for a certain handyman to get some peace and quiet away from her.

Entering first and immediately seeing the ladder in question leaning up against the storage shelf opposite the door, Daisy spotted a jacket hanging on a peg to her other side. Moving slightly to hide the item of clothing from the detective's view with the width of her body, she said cheerily, "There you go, search over."

"Excellent, thank you Vicar," Cluero lifted the folded wooden steps out of the room and Daisy listened for his receding footsteps on the tiled floor as he carried the ladder outside to extend it fully and look for any signs of sabotage other than the damage caused by the fall itself.

Feeling her heart thump loudly in her chest, Daisy quickly examined the jacket which she presumed to be Arthur's, feeling a burst of excitement when she found a mobile phone in the inside pocket. Why she chose to keep this information to herself, Daisy wasn't sure, except to say that she didn't trust Matlock to not implicate her in some way and she knew deep down that she could never focus on finding Gran's killer with the investigation ongoing into two new murders right on her doorstep.

The quicker this was resolved, the better for all concerned. Self-preservation, Daisy convinced herself, was only a part of it.

13. TO SERVE THE PARISH THE BEST I CAN

The phone itself was useless without the pin number to unlock the device, and this Daisy didn't have. Nor had she known Arthur well enough to guess at it. She stabbed in a few combinations of four numbers as she made her way back to the vicarage some twenty minutes later after saying goodbye to Cluero, but of course there were so many possible variations that it was too much of a shot in the dark to prove helpful. Frustrated, Daisy slipped the phone into her pocket hoping that inspiration would strike later, even if it would perhaps necessitate a trip upstairs to Arthur's room. For now, though, she sadly had two funerals to plan. As far as she knew, neither Arthur nor Nora had relatives either inside the town or out, but nevertheless Daisy planned to post the service details in the local paper and on the church noticeboard. Hopefully some kind-hearted parishioners would take some time out of their day in a couple of weeks' time to pay their respects.

"Daisy, Daisy lass!"

Daisy pivoted on her cane to see Joe huffing and puffing up the driveway, past the overgrown graveyard.

"Uncle Joe, this is a lovely surprise."

"Well it wasn't a lovely surprise for me twenty minutes ago, I can tell you! I've just heard lass, from a couple of old biddies in the coffee shop, about the housekeeper. You should've phoned me Daisy, I would've come straight up, you know."

"I know, I know, and I did save your number in my phone the other day. I thought about calling you when I found her, but then things snowballed and I ended up spending the night at Sylvia's house."

"You found the body? Ye gods girl, did that not send you careening right back to that night fifteen years ago?"

"It did."

"Hmm, let's get out of here for an hour or two."

"I have their funerals to plan," she tapped her dog collar absentmindedly.

"Aye, and your own mental health to look after. Come on, we'll take a trip on my bike."

"You came on your Harley?"

"I did, the old hog has a few good years left in her yet. I've got a spare helmet and we'll just go across the bridge to the Crow's Nest Inn for a change of scenery, eh?"

Daisy had to admit that a ride on the bike sounded good, she used to love it when she was younger – much to her grandmother's annoyance, she recalled fondly, "Gran used to call that thing a death trap."

"Well, I'm still here to tell the tale," he stopped suddenly when they both realised the irony in Joe's words – that he was still here but Gran was not.

To avoid him feeling bad for the inadvertent remark, Daisy quickly said, "Let me lock up then and grab my backpack, you've convinced me."

Daisy walked into the bar area of the centuries-old tavern on Joe's arm, since they hadn't found a way yet to accommodate her walking stick safely on the bike. The place hadn't changed in the past two hundred years, and certainly not since Daisy had been away from the town. The walls were still stained yellow and adorned with random horseshoes and old sepia stills, the faux tapestry curtains at the leaded windows were faded and threadbare, and the narrow shelf that ran the length of the walls, just below the ceiling, still looked about to collapse under the weight of the vintage tankards. Daisy took a moment to enjoy the nostalgia as Joe escorted her to a table.

"You sit there lass and I'll get the drinks, what'll it be? Are vicars even allowed to drink any alcohol apart from communion wine?"

"Well, this vicar certainly is," she gave him a wink, "but I'll just have a lager shandy please, since it's still early."

"Right you are," Joe ambled across to the bar, where Daisy thought she recognised the young woman who served him. Having been two years below Daisy in high school, Gemma Sanderson was exactly as Daisy remembered, petite in stature but with wrestler's arms and the ability to down a pint faster than her regulars.

It had been Gemma's father who owned the inn back then, and Daisy wondered if that was still the case. Joe returned with the drinks – a coke for himself since he was driving – just as Gemma looked up to see who he was sitting with.

"Daisy Bloom! My goodness, I wondered when I'd see you! We get to hear all the town news in here, so I knew you were back," Gemma rushed from behind the bar straight to where Daisy sat and enveloped the vicar in a huge hug which Daisy awkwardly tried to return. They had never been close as children, but Daisy had found that people regarded her more fondly in light of her Grandmother's murder. It was mainly pity, to be fair, but Daisy tried not to react angrily to it the way she had used to.

"Yes, back to serve the parish the best I can," Daisy gave her pat response.

"Well, we're lucky to have you, I'm sure," Gemma took the spare chair at their table without asking and settled in as if they were about to have a good old catch-up. Joe caught Daisy's eye and raised an eyebrow, but said nothing, whilst Daisy felt herself physically wilting in her seat at the thought of it. The bar was quiet so no hope of a reprieve from another customer, either.

"Did you hear about Briggs' estate? I mean, it hasn't been announced yet, but with my Paul working up there, I get the inside info so to speak. Did you know I'm married? Yes, coming up for eight years, I'm Gemma Dalton now and co-own this place with my dad, though he's in Gran Canaria on holiday at the mo…" she relayed each sentence as one long stream of consciousness, almost without pausing for breath, so Daisy struggled to stay attentive to the woman, "… so as soon as the council posts the details of the planning consultation we'll be right there, getting our objections noted."

"Don't you agree with the development then?" Daisy asked, not sure if Gemma had mentioned her reasoning and she'd just tuned out.

"Because of Paul's job," Gemma did seem slightly exasperated, but her good nature won through and she set off again, "so, my husband works for Briggs up there, managing the seasonal labourers, crop rotation, all that jazz, did a degree in agricultural management so couldn't have worked out better. Been there for years, only to be told that this development will be moving away from traditional farming and into the luxury tourism and global wellness sector so there'll no longer be a role for him. I mean, can you imagine?"

Daisy could feel that her eyes had glazed over again, and was about to respond, when they were saved by the arrival of a new customer. Or so Daisy thought, until she saw that the newcomer was Rob Briggs of all people. Gemma clamped her mouth shut and made her way back behind the counter, all the while shooting daggers at the back of the man waiting to be served. Turning to look for the barmaid, and then seeing the table she had just vacated, Rob's face broke into a wide smile and he immediately strode over to join them.

"Dee-Dee, Uncle Joe, can I get you both another round?"

"No thanks," Daisy quickly replied, "no rest for the wicked." She spotted Joe's questioning gaze but ignored it. He and Rob had always been friendly when she was dating the younger version of the man now standing in front of her, despite Joe's feelings for the boy's father. She couldn't face any more reminiscing right now, though, so made it clear they wouldn't be staying long enough for him to join them.

"Ah well, another time perhaps? Soon, Daisy? I need all the excuses I can get to escape dad at the moment."

"Of course," Daisy repented the white lie the moment she said it but even God knew, sometimes needs must.

"Has your father changed his mind yet?" Daisy heard Gemma ask Rob as she stood to leave.

"You know how stubborn the old man is," Rob replied, shaking his head sympathetically, "once he sees the pound signs in a project he's like a dog with a bone. I've tried to persuade him, really."

Gemma tut-tutted her disapproval as she poured the man's pint of ale and Daisy wondered to herself how much Rob had been at loggerheads with Briggs Senior since his return to Lillymouth. Certainly, she knew that the two men had rarely seen eye to eye when she and Rob were teenagers. Daisy's Gran had rented a field up at the farm complete with polytunnels and a couple of greenhouses, and she and Daisy had spent a lot of time up there growing flowers and plants to sell in the shop. That place had been the location for a few heady trysts in the distant past, too, though Daisy pushed those memories from her mind.

"Has the bloke done anything to upset you, or do you just not want to revisit the past?" Joe asked as they walked back to his motorbike.

"No, nothing specific, I just... I'm worried he wants to take up where we left off and that is very much, definitely off the table. Besides, you know my history here, it's hard enough fitting back in without making things more complicated."

"I understand, lass, and for what it's worth I agree. I think this whole development thing will get messy when all the details are formally announced and it'll be better for the vicar not to be seen to be taking sides."

"Exactly," Daisy let out a sigh of relief. She didn't need approval or to feel validated, yet it felt nice when it came.

Changing the subject as he handed her the spare helmet, Joe's voice was deeper and gruffer as he said, "Wendy loved riding this thing, you know?"

"Gran? No! She always warned me off it!"

"I know, she was just thinking of your safety, but when it was just the two of us..." he trailed off, deep in his memories.

"I guess there's a lot about her, as a person rather than as my grandmother, that I didn't know," Daisy said, with the clarity and comprehension that only comes with age.

Joe merely smiled, and Daisy got the distinct impression there was a lot he wasn't telling her.

14. JUST PHOTOS

It had been a long few days since Nora's death and Daisy was just about to run herself a well-deserved bubble bath. Seeing her close her laptop on the kitchen table, Jacob stretched his paws and arched his back, waking from his fifth nap of the day, and jumped down to follow Daisy upstairs to the only bathroom. Woefully in need of a lot more than simple redecoration, this room still sported an original toilet complete with pull chain and a roll-top bath that had no doubt seen better days in the very dim and distant past. It was far from ideal for Daisy, having to haul herself up the extremely narrow and steep staircase every time she needed to use the facilities. What was worse, though, was that it had taken all of Daisy's courage to come up here after Nora's death, and still every time she did so it was with not a small amount of trepidation.

Almost tripping over the cat who was right behind her at the top of the stairs when she decided to pop into Arthur's old bedroom before going into the bathroom, Daisy bent slowly to pick up Jacob, her back protesting loudly as she scooped the overly large feline into her arms.

"Come on Jacob, I could do with some company," Daisy whispered, refusing to dwell on the fact she was becoming attached to the animal.

Pushing open the door slowly, Daisy walked quickly to the shelf above Arthur's old desk where she had left his mobile phone. She had deposited it here the other day after having had no luck unlocking it, and had only just on the spur of the moment plucked up the courage to do a bit of digging.

Seeing the comfortable bed, still made neatly as Arthur had left it despite the break in which had left the opposite half of the room ransacked, Jacob jumped from Daisy's arms to find a cosy vantage point. Relieved her hands were now free of the cumbersome weight, Daisy picked up the phone and whispered to herself, *Think Daisy, think logically. He was a simple man, with simple pleasures. Church, the town... Lizzie! He loved*

Lizzie Briggs.

As far as Daisy could recall, the pair were trying to keep their amorous relationship private, though from what she had heard it was the worst kept secret in the town. Nevertheless, whilst Arthur may not have wanted to flaunt it publicly, Daisy was sure he must've had some personal tokens and reminders of his and Lizzie's love. Feeling slightly guilty for prying, but telling herself it was for the greater good that justice for Arthur and Nora might be served, Daisy began looking through the man's belongings. She sifted through the mess left on the floor first – the things the police hadn't bothered to take – and found nothing of note. Old copies of the 'Lillymouth Echo,' art supplies, parish newsletters from the church services, nothing particularly personal. Daisy abandoned this, getting slowly back to her feet, and deciding she might have more luck on the side of the room that hadn't been trashed. Presumably Nora had interrupted the intruder before they had a chance to empty Arthur's bedside table which, other than the bed, was the only piece of furniture on this side.

Jacob gave a reassuring meow and purred as Daisy sat beside him and stroked the cat's head, bolstering herself for what she considered to be the invasion of privacy she was about to carry out. Gingerly, she pulled open the first of two drawers in the wooden unit. As with the top of the cabinet, this contained nothing that jumped out to the vicar as useful. A couple of books on local history, an encyclopedia of Yorkshire birds and their chosen habitats, a notebook with vague scribbles detailing birds personally spotted by the deceased man, a pencil and an empty glasses case. Daisy sighed in defeat, hardly paying attention as she opened the second and last drawer.

As soon as she looked down, however, and saw the framed photograph, Daisy felt the small burst of excitement that told her she had discovered something different. Something altogether more personal. Gently lifting the metal frame from where it was nestled on top of what looked to be a lady's scarf, Daisy saw that it contained a photo of Arthur with Lizzie Briggs. The two looked to be in a restaurant, and a cake sat on the table in front of Lizzie with 'Happy Birthday' iced across the top. Hoping desperately that there would be a date stamp, Daisy found that very thing in the bottom corner of the picture. Half obscured by the frame, she had to gently remove it to see the full date, March twelfth.

Her heart beating faster, her breathing shallower, Daisy quickly typed 1203 into the mobile phone and felt a jolt of energy course through her as the pin number unlocked the device. Even Jacob, clearly sensing the change in mood, opened one eye to look disdainfully at the screen in Daisy's hand. A picture of Arthur, again with Lizzie Briggs, but this time taken from a high vantage point with the land to the south of the Lillywater river behind them – *from the steeple tower?* Daisy wondered – greeted her as the phone's screensaver.

Daisy knew she should hand this in to the police as evidence. Moreover, she was aware that she now had more of a moral quandary to face – how much of the man's personal messages and files should she dig into? Daisy said a prayer and waited for some kind of divine reply. When nothing came other than the nuzzling of the fat cat next to her demanding to be stroked, Daisy knew she had to make this decision herself, based on her own conscience.

"Just photos," she said to Jacob, as if wanting some reassurance that her judgement was sound, "they can't be too personal, can they? Then we can leave the emails, contact numbers and such for the police. Yes, a good compromise."

Totally uninterested, the cat closed his eyes again, his whiskers tickling Daisy's wrist where his head snuggled against her.

There were very few pictures in the camera roll from the past couple of months – after Lizzie's untimely death, Daisy presumed. Before that, though, there were many pictures of the couple out and about on hikes along the coastal path and around the town. There were more pictures clearly taken on the same day as the screensaver, from up high looking out over the town with Briggs' farm – Lizzie's home with her brother – in the distance and then zoomed in more closely. There were plenty of photos of plants and birds, nothing that jumped out. Daisy sighed and decided she had pried into the dead man's affairs enough for one day. She went to click off the file, but this was an older and different make and model to Daisy's own phone so instead of taking her back to the homepage, she was presented with a list of files within the photos app. One in particular, titled simply 'Liz' stood out. Hoping she wouldn't find pictures of an extremely personal nature, Daisy was relieved to see they were merely shots in and around Briggs' farm. Close ups of the outhouses and barns, both inside and out, which Lizzie must've taken and forwarded to her beau. Other than hay lofts and old machinery, however, Daisy wasn't sure what the photos were meant to be showing.

The doorbell rang twice at that very moment causing

Daisy to jump guiltily as if she had been caught red-handed doing something she shouldn't. Jacob jolted awake angrily and hissed in the direction of the bedroom door, whilst Daisy heard Archie pipe up from downstairs with his usual, "Not today, thank you."

Daisy was inclined to agree with the bird, given that it was seven in the evening and she had just been about to run a bath. The hammering continued, however, and Daisy slipped the phone into the drawer along with the photo, closed it and made her way slowly downstairs, noticing that Jacob had refused to budge for the unexpected visitors.

15. UNORTHODOX HABITS

As Robert Briggs Senior pushed past her into the vicarage, Daisy felt the sudden urge to tell the man to leave before she had even heard what he had come for. The vicar was silenced before her mouth could form the words, however, when she saw the line of people filing up the path behind the man. Panicking for a moment, that they had come to do some kind of parishioners revolt and tell her they wanted her out, Daisy simply stood back meekly as the eight high-profile locals walked past her without as much as a greeting and went straight into the kitchen.

"What can I do for you?" Daisy asked, closing the door and following the last of them into the now cramped room.

Briggs gave her a look of scorn, as if he thought Daisy very simple minded, and replied, "The parish council meeting, once a month."

"Yes, what of it? I admit, with the two murders I've been focusing on I haven't had a chance to become as quickly acquainted with the church calendar as I would've liked, so if I've missed a meeting then I apol…"

"No, woman, this is the parish council meeting. You did tell her, Violet, didn't you?"

Violet Glendinning sent a hooded smirk in Daisy's direction, "It must have slipped my mind, Robert."

"What? Here? In the vicarage kitchen?" Daisy couldn't quite get her head around it, though everyone else sat down on either side of the table, with those that wouldn't fit standing beside the counter, as if this was the normal way of things.

"Yes dear," Martha Bridges, wife of the local councillor said kindly, "your predecessor preferred to do away with the formality of meetings and such, and instead he baked cakes once a month and we came here for a quick chat about what was happening in the parish over a cuppa."

Things began to become clearer in Daisy's mind now, "Ah, I see, thank you Mrs. Bridges. So," and this she directed at Robert Briggs, "Reverend Martin took a back seat in the handling of parish affairs, in return for what… perhaps you overlooking some of his more, ah, unorthodox habits?"

"I don't know what you mean!" Violet's voice was shrill and grated on Daisy's nerves.

"Then let me spell it out more clearly," Daisy tried not to grind her teeth as she spoke slowly and forcefully, "from next month these meetings will resume in the parish hall, where they should be. They will be minuted and all proposals and decisions formally recorded."

Briggs coughed and blustered, while Violet Glendinning couldn't help herself but spew an angry retort, "Well, if you wish things to be on a more formal footing, vicar, then I suggest you forgo the denim dresses and ridiculous bright tunics in favour of more conventional attire. The same could be said for that hideous multi-coloured walking sti…"

"Violet!" Martha Bridges cut in, "Must things get so personal?"

"Thank you, Martha," Daisy took a slow deep breath in

through her nose and out through her mouth, feeling all eyes on her. The Lord must surely be with her now, she thought, since Daisy had not felt this much confidence and surety in her position since arriving back in Lillymouth, "Mrs. Glendinning, personal affronts will get you nowhere other than my recommendation that you stand down as chair of this council. As the ordained member of the clergy assigned to the beautiful parish of Lillymouth, I am now in charge of arranging all meetings pertaining to the church and the ecumenical side of parish business. And I can assure you, that changes… Will. Be. Made."

Violet looked about to retort, her thin visage having turned an unbecoming shade of puce, but she was silenced by the loud beeping of what sounded like a smoke detector.

"Is there a fire?" Martha asked shakily above the din, her face having become instantly pale.

Daisy had an idea what the real source of the noise was – or rather, who – but it served her purpose to perpetuate the idea that they should all evacuate the building, so that is what she hurriedly suggested.

To the sound of many grumbles and the claim that 'they hadn't even been given a cup of tea for their trouble,' the group filed out, with Daisy assuring them that she would arrange another meeting, in the parish hall this time, very soon.

Funnily enough, the shrill noise stopped the moment they were all outside, and Daisy caught the flutter of feathers out of the corner of her eye as the small black bird flew into the room they had all just vacated. From her spot on the front step, the sudden silence allowed Daisy to hear a small excerpt of the conversation between Violet Glendinning and Robert Briggs...

"Aye, it's less than a week now till the cut-off for the planning objections, then I have it on good authority everything will be approved without delay..." Briggs said assuredly.

That can't be right, Daisy thought to herself, as she closed the door and made sure to lock it securely, *Gemma and her husband have been looking out for that consultation to be made public, as is the legal requirement, so how has it only days left?* Daisy had an idea how it might have happened, perhaps involving a more unscrupulous planning officer and an exchange of money – she certainly wouldn't put it past Briggs Senior to use bribery or worse, blackmail, to get what he wanted – but this was purely conjecture and hard evidence would be needed if she were to make this accusation public. *Certainly,* Daisy concluded, *the future of the land up at Briggs' farm is somehow tied up in all of this – not least, the two murders right here on church property.*

For the way he had treated her grandmother, and his attitude towards Daisy now, she was determined to find out all there was to know about Robert Briggs Senior. *If that exposes him as a murderer, then all the better.*

16. BOUNTIFUL BLOOMS

Daisy had forgotten about the house rabbit.

She was now the unfortunate silent witness to a standoff worthy of a showdown at the O.K. Corral. The newcomer, Malone, was standing at the end of the downstairs corridor next to Daisy's bedroom, whilst Jacob had taken up position at the other end, in front of the kitchen door. Archie had flown up to perch almost halfway between the two on the top of the sitting room door like some sort of dark adjudicator, and all three now eyed each other suspiciously.

"Bugsy Malone, get your stompers up those stairs and we'll get your little bed made up all cosy like," Sylvia said, coming in through the front door with an armful of bedding. She passed Daisy at the foot of the narrow staircase and whispered, "he's just showing off to his new friends."

'Friends' was a bit of a push, Daisy thought, but she smiled and nodded as she made her way out of the front door for the third time and slowly down to her car to collect more of the belongings they'd just brought up from Sylvia's.

"I've got a lad with a van coming with the bigger stuff tomorrow. Are you sure you're happy to put my sofas in the sitting room and move these older pieces of furniture across to the church? I don't want to invade your space completely, petal, I feel bad enough using Nora's room so soon after her passing," Sylvia asked when they were seated at the kitchen table with a well-earned cup of tea. Jacob sat possessively on Daisy's lap, deliberately purring loud enough to wake the dead, whilst Malone hopped around sniffing out his new surroundings.

"No, really, I'm absolutely sure. I'll ask Joe to help me move the wingback chairs to my office in the church. It'll be much cosier here with your squishy sofas and cushions, thank you Sylvia, you're doing me a favour."

"No Daisy, I'll never forget what you're doing for me. Anything you need help with, anything at all, you've

116

just got to say the word."

"Actually, Sylvia, now that you mention it, I recall you saying you help out in the town hall sometimes?"

"Aye, every Monday and Thursday mornings. It being the same building on the town square as the library, I move about between the different departments depending on where they need me."

"Perfect, would you be able then to take a little detour to the planning department when you're in tomorrow?" Daisy elaborated on the information she needed and felt not an ounce of guilt about it. After all, she simply wished to share what should be public knowledge with the residents of Lillymouth. Who could find fault with that?

"Say no more, it's as good as done," Sylvia said, eying the cat who was now rubbing his head on the underside of Daisy's chin, "and, if you don't mind me asking, lass, what've you been feeding this furry lump here? He smells awfully fishy like."

"Who, Jacob? Well, I ran out of the tins of cat food that Nora had left in the cupboard of the boot room, but there was a stack of tuna here in the kitchen pantry, so he's been getting through four tins of that a day. Must be starving poor thing, the speed at which he gobbles it up. Why? Do you think he needs more?"

"More? Goodness heavens no, you aren't used to pets are you, Vicar? No wonder the cat has taken a quick liking to you!"

"Well no, is it that obvious? There were bird food pellets for the mynah bird in his cage, so I've been topping those up. He is an unusual species though, so maybe we should search online to see what else he likes?" It was all starting to feel a bit like a petting zoo, but Daisy didn't say so for fear of hurting Sylvia's feelings. A house rabbit though? Daisy thought that may be a step too far, before telling herself that she already had guardianship of a mynah bird, of all things!

"You leave it to me, Daisy, you've enough on your hands, I'll feed them at the same time as my Malone, and maybe we can get that cat to leave the house for some exercise."

"You'll be lucky," Daisy said, well aware how hard it was to even budge the creature from her knee these days.

Daisy left Sylvia to unpack and spent the afternoon in

her office at the church. 'Office' was probably an overly generous description of what appeared to be a converted cupboard. Now that she'd sat at the desk and taken a closer look at the space, Daisy realised neither of the large chairs from the vicarage would fit in here.

Perhaps a gift to a home for the elderly? Daisy mused as she sifted through the piles of papers strewn across the table in front of her. To say her predecessor had not been organised was an understatement. Letters from the Bishop mixed with body building magazines, bills for enough energy drinks to keep a football team moving were next to orders of service. It was a mess, and one which Daisy was tempted to simply bag up and bin. Nevertheless, she spent three hours sorting and filing, shredding and diarising, until everything was neat and in order ready for her to start afresh. Whilst her mind calmed at the now-clear space, Daisy's back however protested loudly, and the all-too-familiar pains shot down her left side.

Standing to stretch, Daisy decided a change of scene would be beneficial, and hoped a few minutes of prayer in the main chapel of the church would provide inspiration for her next sermon.

"Vicar Bloom!" Daisy jumped as the familiar booming

tones of Gerald Bunch assailed her before she'd even fully entered the space. Had she clocked him first, you can be sure she would have beat a hasty and silent retreat. As it was, Daisy had been spotted and had no choice but to engage in conversation with the odious man.

"Reverend Daisy is fine," she said, trying to assume a confident air.

"Fine indeed!" Bunch replied, licking his lips in that awfully distasteful manner he had, "And how is our voluptuous vicar this beautiful day?"

Ignoring both the blatant double meaning and the more overt reference to her figure, Daisy swallowed the feeling of nausea that this man evoked and instead focused her gaze on the beautiful flower arrangement he was just finishing, "I didn't know you did the church flowers personally, Mr. Bunch."

"Gerald, please, and yes, it is one of my favourite times of the week. Quiet and peaceful."

The idea of seeking peace and quiet seemed to jar with what Daisy knew of the man's personality, but she simply nodded, "Well, I and the parishioners thank you. Perhaps now would be a good time to discuss the flowers for the upcoming funerals?"

"Yes, sad business indeed. What an awful start to your time here, Vicar. Please let me know any ways in which I can, ah, soothe your transition." He drew out the word 'soothe' making it sound a lot more salacious than the word itself normally implied.

And the nausea was back again, full force this time.

Daisy's ears were ringing from the fact the man simply couldn't seem to speak in any other volume than extremely loud, and her palms were becoming sweaty from the need to get away from him.

Plastering a weak smile on her face, the best she could muster under the circumstances, Daisy said, "I don't think either Arthur or Nora had relatives so something simple for the top of the coffins…"

"Say no more, Vicar, it will be my pleasure to provide these, free of charge."

"Oh! Well, there's no need, I mean, the church doesn't like to be in debt to…" and she certainly didn't want to be in debt to him personally.

"Aren't we all called to serve in whatever capacity we can?" He chuckled, in the way of someone who knows they have won an argument.

"Indeed, thank you, Mr. Bunch, I should be going,"

Daisy took three steps forward, the taps of her cane echoing off the parquet floor, before she decided now was as good a time as any to ask a question that had been bothering her since her return, "Ah, just before I do, I was wondering why you chose to keep my grandmother's name for the florist shop?"

If he was surprised by the question, Bunch hid it very well. His large, hooded eyes merely blinked twice behind his thinly framed spectacles, perched precariously on his almost unnaturally thin nose, and he spoke with the same hearty assurance as ever, "Who would want to change such a beautiful and perfectly appropriate name, Vicar? 'Bountiful Blooms' had such a good reputation, and well, just seemed to speak to me. I hope you don't mind."

"Not at all, Mr. Bunch, it must have spoken to you rather loudly, since you paid so much over the odds for the building."

For the first time, the man opposite her appeared wrongfooted and his gaze turned stony for the briefest of moments before returning to his usual intensely amorous leer, "It was a long time ago, Vicar. I mean look at you, all grown up and womanly."

And he'd done it again. Managed to turn the conversation to increase Daisy's discomfort, meaning she had no intention of spending a minute longer in the man's presence. It was definitely a skill that he had, and Daisy decided she'd need to be better armed against it in future.

17. A BIRD'S EYE VIEW

"It was kind of you to invite me round for a meal, Uncle Joe, I ate with Sylvia last night as it was her first evening in the vicarage, but, well, she likes to chat, and I think I've become too used to my own company."

"Completely understand, I don't even converse with my regulars much these days, salty old sea dog that I am. But don't be too excited, it's just fish and chips from along the promenade there. I did remember you like mushy peas, though," he smiled sadly over the paper-wrapped package that contained their meal, "just like your Gran."

"It's perfect Joe, really, I haven't had a decent fish and chip takeaway in years. Smells delicious too," Daisy sat back on the leather recliner, the only 'proper' chair in the place, and admired the artwork on the walls of Joe's small lounge as he plated up their meal. What it lacked in square footage, the room made up for with a large picture window that looked straight onto the beach and sea beyond. At this time of day, with the sun low in the sky casting a gentle glow and the waves calm for once, the almost-deserted beach was like a golden paradise.

"I could look out at that view for hours and never be bored," Daisy sighed in contentment as she finished her last bite of the deliciously greasy fare they'd eaten on trays on their lap.

"Aye, I find it puts most things into perspective," Joe said.

"Though not all," Daisy whispered, and she knew they were both thinking about Gran again. It seemed impossible not to when they were in each other's company. Daisy suspected Joe could do with closure even more than she could – the intervening years seemed to have done nothing to dampen his affections towards the woman he had lost.

Shaking his head as if to dispel depressing thoughts, Joe reached behind the old deckchair on which he was sitting and produced a framed picture, "Now Daisy, I wanted to get you something like a welcome home present, you know, to let you know how glad I am you're here, but ah, I'm not good with things like that. I mainly just know about the tides, how to make a decent coffee, and then there's my painting hobby. I took it up after the… after she… well, just after you left as the doctor thought it would be a form of art therapy. Anyway, what I'm trying to say is that I did what I know best and painted a watercolour of the town for you. It's not professional or anythi…"

"Joe! Oh my goodness, let me see," Daisy reached out and took the large frame from him, turning it the right way around and balancing it on her knee. She was speechless.

"I told you it's not that good," Joe said to fill the silence, which had begun to stretch awkwardly between them.

"No, I," Daisy paused to swallow down the lump in her throat. She could barely see the painting now through eyes blurred with tears, "I love it, Joe, thank you, it's a beautiful angle from above, like a bird's eye view."

The moment she had said it, Daisy's brain flicked to other, more photographic images of the town from above. Those she had found on Arthur's camera. And the mention of birds…

"Aye, and it's all there," Joe continued, oblivious to Daisy's change in focus, "the church, the little primary school, the two bridges over the river, the old station and twin piers…"

"And the farm," Daisy noted, studying the picture before her once again, "it must've taken you ages, Joe, thank you so much."

"Aye well, I've worked on it on and off over the years in the hope that I'd get to give it to you in person one day."

Daisy propped the picture gently against the wall and rose slowly. She leaned over and pecked Joe on the cheek, causing the man to become visibly embarrassed, "Thank you," she whispered.

"Aye well, the view won't look like that for much longer, so maybe it'll be worth something in the future," Joe deliberately broke the emotional moment and Daisy was grateful.

Taking the opportunity to change the subject onto something less personal, she replied, "And that's the shame of it. A centuries-old landscape will be irrevocably changed if Briggs' plans go ahead. Not to mention the divide it will cause – I know Bea's husband, Andrew, is relying on a contract from the new build, whilst as you heard Gemma's husband at the inn will lose his job. I'm sure there'll be many more cases like these, separating the townsfolk into those for and against. It can't be good, can it?"

"Certainly not for a vicar trying to promote harmony and togetherness," Joe joked, but Daisy could tell he was angry about the development, "I'm not averse to change, Daisy, but not at any cost. And besides, who will it attract to the town? Not your average tourist, that's for sure. The people Briggs will be targeting will have in-house chefs and organised day trips in chauffeur-driven cars, they won't be spending their wads of cash in little coffee shops like mine and Bea's."

"I know, that's what I'm afraid of. And what lengths will the man go to to get what he wants?"

"Now that there, that's the million dollar question, isn't it," Joe stood to put the kettle on, leaving Daisy with her troubling thoughts.

What lengths indeed? And did they include murder?

When Daisy let herself back into the vicarage a short

while later she was immediately assailed by the plaintive meows of the large ginger tom cat, who curled around her ankles almost tripping her up.

"Now Jacob, come on, you must be hungry."

"He most certainly is not," Sylvia's voice floated through from the kitchen, "he's had his allotted cat food for the day, so don't you be giving him anything extra, not even a little treat, do you hear?"

"Yes Sylvia," Daisy couldn't hide the smile in her voice. She hadn't been mothered like this since Gran. To the cat she whispered, "Sorry, I've been overruled."

As if sensing her refusal, the feisty feline turned his back to her, his rear end high and haughty, and stalked off to make himself comfortable on the vicar's pillow.

"I've a brew going," Sylvia said as Daisy entered the kitchen, sitting herself at the table beside the offered mug of tea.

"Thank you," Daisy tried to hide her yawn behind her hand.

"Not been getting enough sleep have you," it was a statement rather than a question, "it'll be all the to-do with these murders, no doubt."

"Ah, yes, troubling times since I've been back," Daisy replied, caught up in her own thoughts, "you know Sylvia, I think Briggs' development is the key to this whole thing. Oh! Did you have any luck at the planning department?"

"Well, I spoke to my old friend Lydia, she's the secretary there you know, lost her husband about the same time as me but has two grown up daughters and three beautiful grandchildren to keep her busy…"

Daisy tried to stay looking interested, but must've failed, as Sylvia stopped short, "Sorry vicar, ah the plans, yes, they were announced almost two weeks back, but apparently the council legally has discretion over how they advertise these public consultations. Depending on the type of planning proposal, they have different obligations, but the basic two are to announce the consultation on their website and in the local press."

"And have they done that?" Daisy clasped her hands together on top of the table.

"Ah, yes and no. It seems the announcement in the Lillymouth Echo was a tiny piece, buried at the back amongst adverts for slimming clubs and dating sites. The article on the website appears to have been 'mistakenly' posted in the local sports clubs section which is still under construction. A rather convenient error, don't you think?"

"Convenient indeed. So, Briggs paid someone to bury it."

"I would say so. Lydia says there's notes on the file to say a poster has been put up at the end of the farthest pier, on the lighthouse, and another in the disused waiting room at the old train station. So, no hope in hell of anyone seeing them there. It seems someone is so far in Briggs' pocket they can no longer smell the sea air," Sylvia finished, shaking her head in disapproval and topping up her cup with hot tea from the pot.

"And now the time for objections is running out," Daisy said dejectedly.

"Aye, time's slipping away to get this stopped, that's for sure."

"It's not over yet, though," Daisy said, straightening her back and setting her mug down decisively, "I may have had a bit of a breakthrough over at Joe's so I'm going to do some investigating tomorrow. Would you have time to come to the library with me?"

"Ooh, like a private investigator? I'm in!" Sylvia said, with decidedly more glee than Daisy felt the situation warranted.

Nevertheless, the vicar smiled and tried to grasp onto the small flicker of hope in her chest. If Robert Briggs thought he could buy or bury any opposition to his proposed development, then he had a shock coming.

18. AN OVERSIZED, BOUNCY BED INVADER

Daisy shot up to a seated position, banging her head on the wooden headboard as she did so and biting down on the expletives which almost tumbled forth. As if her bad dreams with flashbacks from her argument with Gran the day before her death were not enough, opening her eyes to be confronted with a white rabbit only inches from her face was quite a scare in itself. When she'd put the small stepladder beside her bed to aid with getting her stiff leg up in the morning, Daisy hadn't envisaged it being used by an oversized, bouncy bed invader. As Daisy became suddenly aware of her surroundings, she clocked the arched back of the hissing cat at the foot of the bed, the rabbit ensconced on the pillow beside her studying her quizzically, and the mynah bird on top of the curtain pole who, on making eye contact with the vicar, began imitating an alarm clock.

"No, no, no," Daisy said firmly, rubbing the sleep out of her eyes, "from now on you'll be shut into the kitchen overnight, all of you!"

Her threats went unheeded, however, as cat and rabbit were too engrossed in their latest standoff, and Archie was ratcheting up the volume. Huffing, Daisy gingerly left her bed, trying to ignore the pain in her body and her mind's immediate thoughts of prescription pain medication.

Dressed and with the largest mug of coffee she could find in her hand, Daisy's first port of call was to Arthur's old bedroom. She flicked through the photos on the deceased man's phone once again, noting his interest in the outbuildings at Briggs' farm and promising herself that she would hand it over to Cluero that day – the police hadn't been back in contact, so Daisy presumed these murders were perhaps not getting the attention they deserved. She then put the device aside in favour of looking more closely at the few books in his bedside drawer. It was the studies on local birds that interested Daisy the most, though she wasn't sure what exactly she was looking for. As far as she could tell, the information was very general in nature and not the more detailed focus on the rarer North Yorkshire species that Daisy wanted.

Back in her bedroom, a quick online search on her laptop also failed to provide Daisy with the swift and definitive answers she needed. There was too much information to sift through, given the current time constraints she was under and her lack of any foundation knowledge on the subject.

Finally, about half an hour later, Daisy heard Sylvia stir upstairs. The woman was a bit of a night owl and therefore definitely not an early riser. Daisy tried to curb her impatience by doing her morning prayers and reading some scripture. Even so, when the older woman finally made an appearance, dressed to the nines and with a full face of makeup, Daisy's good humour was all but gone. Not least when she realised that she herself hadn't even bothered to brush her hair which was still in the previous day's braid.

"Right lass, we'll just have a quick cuppa, shall we? Then we'll be off out to the library," Sylvia started towards the kitchen but Daisy had other plans.

"Let me treat you to tea and cake at Bea's – after the library," she added, helping her friend into her coat purposefully.

The Lillymouth town library, like so many these days, had been shrunk to reflect the public's growing preference for web-based learning and ebooks. Nevertheless, there was a small section on birds, but nothing that gave any more information than the books in Arthur's room. If only Daisy had wanted to learn more about owls, budgies, or how to make the perfect garden feeder then she would've been sorted.

Sylvia, however, had shunned actual book research in favour of having a chat with her former colleague, Rosemary. At first rather put out and indignant, Daisy could've kissed the woman when her lodger came back with a list of the books that either Arthur or Lizzie had borrowed from the library before their tragic deaths. Quite a few didn't provide any insight into the current issue, ranging from 'Yorkshire's Top Twenty Coastal Walks' to 'Over Fifty and Fruity – Fulfilling Your Intimate Desires.' Daisy shuddered as she firmly crossed that one off the list. Funnily enough, there weren't any on birds either, rather the couple had seemed more interested in the broader topic of local wildlife and habitats.

Sylvia was clearly getting antsy and ready to make the short walk along The Parade to Bea's Book Nook, and Daisy could hardly blame her, given the fact she'd prevented the woman from having any breakfast. Scanning the list one last time, Daisy's eye caught on something she had missed on the first pass. One book had the main title 'Preserving our Local Habitats,' but then the subtitle read, 'Spotlight on Bats.' It was that last word that thankfully caught Daisy's eye, just as she was about to write the visit off as a waste of time.

Bats, bats, bats, Daisy chanted to herself as they hurried along to the bookshop, *maybe it's not birds at all.* She struggled to keep up with Sylvia, who for a woman of her age couldn't half get a move on when tea and cake were the motivator. Out of breath and feeling the sweat running down her forehead, Daisy could only imagine the delightful image she presented as they entered the cool, dark interior of her friend's shop.

"Daisy! And Mrs. Carmichael, what a lovely surprise!" As always Bea seemed genuinely happy to see her, which Daisy knew was mostly due to their close relationship, but seeing the tea nook yet again empty Daisy wondered how well her friend's business was actually faring. She made a point of asking Bea to order in some theology books she had been wanting, despite the fact they would've been cheaper online, and then re-joined Sylvia on a squishy leather sofa in the back corner.

Daisy understood that warm days like this one attracted visitors to the beach, but surely locals still popped out for a hot drink in the summer months? Sipping her latte and only half listening to Bea as she showed Sylvia the baby monitor which she used to keep an eye on baby Daisy Mae who was napping in their flat upstairs, Daisy couldn't help but feel bad for her friend. Now that she looked closely, although the books were arranged so as to cover the spaces, in reality only two thirds of the shelves were filled with stock. There had been a loyalty card on the counter, she had noticed, where if you bought five books you got a free coffee, so her friend was clearly trying different marketing techniques to get the customers in, yet the bell over the door hadn't rung once the whole time they'd been there.

Then there was the cake. Daisy tried hard not to be judgemental, but given her train of thought it was understandable that she noticed the carrot cake had turned hard and stale in places, as if it was a couple of days past its best, another indication that there hadn't been enough customers in to eat it. It pained Daisy to think that her friend might be struggling, especially since she and Andrew had just had their first child.

"So," Daisy said, when there was a lull in conversation, trying hard to muster the tact and sensitivity that went hand in hand with her vocation, "ah, how is Andrew getting on? I imagine he's excited for the new contract he told me about, the one up at Briggs' new development?" *Subtle, Daisy, very subtle.*

"What? Oh, ah," Bea seemed to fumble her words, no doubt from the unexpected change in topic, "well, yes, he's just finishing up a small job down the coast and then he has nothing lined up. He's kept his calendar free for the local work he's been promised up at the farm."

Daisy's stomach dropped when she realised how heavily the couple were clearly relying on that large project. She wasn't quite sure what to say, though anything would've been preferable to what Sylvia came out with.

"Well, if I were you I'd tell him to start putting the feelers out elsewhere," Sylvia said confidently, tapping Bea on the arm to emphasise her point, "Briggs' shady dealings may be about to be forced into the light."

"What? Oh no, I don't think there's anything shady," Bea's eyes filled with unshed tears and Daisy quickly intervened.

"I think what Sylvia meant was, it's never a good idea to put all your eggs in one basket," she shot a look at the older woman, who looked suitably regretful.

"Aye, I was just repeating local gossip lass, pay me no heed."

"What if there aren't any other baskets to put our eggs in?" Bea asked, sinking down into the chair next to them from having been perched on the arm of their sofa, "I mean, Andrew's looked, near and far, but the work isn't there at the moment, or else bigger firms are undercutting him whenever he tenders a quote. And I'm hardly raking it in here. This old Victorian pile has its charms in winter, with no windows down this end of the shop so just the fairy lights and the real fire roaring, people find it cosy and charming. At this time of year, not so much. It's stuffy and dark." She shrugged her shoulders in a gesture of defeat.

"Oh Bea, I'm sorry, we must do something, a fundraiser or bake off, I'm not sure. Something to get people in though."

"Perhaps," Bea smiled wanly and stood as they heard the baby upstairs begin to fuss.

Daisy crushed a twenty pound note into her friend's hand as they said their goodbyes. Far more than the total of the bill, but she felt guilty for having brought further sadness and gloom to her friend's day.

Forget council departments, planning permission and bribes, it was the real people of the town who would suffer one way or another as a result of Robert Briggs' actions.

And that was before you even considered the murders.

19. A CASE OF MISTAKEN IDENTITY

The time had come for more decisive action, Daisy decided upon their return to the vicarage, as she left Sylvia making a chicken salad for lunch and slipped back upstairs to Arthur's room. The walk back up Cobble Wynd had taken twice as long as necessary – even considering Daisy's slower pace – as Sylvia knew everyone in the town and stopped to speak to most that she passed. Daisy was aware that, as the new vicar, she should be paying attention to names and family relationships, but her mind was firmly elsewhere. She wasted no time, therefore, the moment they were back home, from hurrying to get the mobile phone from Arthur's bedside table.

Whilst a regard for the man's privacy had prevented the vicar from looking at Arthur's emails thus far, she now felt the move was justified if it helped find the poor man's killer. A few minutes of concentrated prayer left Daisy none the wiser as to whether God blessed her actions – she felt neither calm resolve nor uncomfortable regret – though she was pretty sure the Bishop would disapprove. Daisy knew she could leave it to the professionals, of course, but the image of Detective Michelle Matlock sneering as Daisy fumbled her way through talk of bats and landscape pictures was enough to put her firmly off that course of action.

No, Daisy would take the matter into her own hands.

Once past the first pin number, the mobile device thankfully had no further password protection and Daisy could move around the different apps at will. Opening the single email account with a shortcut on the home screen, Daisy's eyes honed in on the most recent message, sitting at the top of the list, sent the day of Arthur's death but as yet unopened. It was from a company called The Ecology Partnership, and Daisy's heart began to beat faster as she clicked to view its contents.

Daisy read the message twice to be sure she had her facts straight before pulling her own phone out of her pocket and dialling the number at the top of the letter. Greetings dispensed with quickly, Daisy hurried to the main crux of her call.

"Thank you, yes, I'm the vicar here in Lillymouth. I believe you may have been in contact with Arthur Smith? I have your email to him here, and I'm sad to say the poor man passed away just before you sent it."

"Oh my goodness," the kind woman on the other end replied, "let me check our records… Yes, we have been in contact with an Elizabeth Briggs and Mr. Smith for several months now. After some discussions a few months back with one of our experts, they requested a bat survey at the lady's property to confirm that there were roosts in the outbuildings which by law cannot be disturbed, even if there are no bats currently present in them. It took just under two months for their application to come to the top of the fast-track pile and be passed to our team who considered all the evidence they sent. It was therefore just over a week ago that I phoned the number given by Ms. Briggs to provide an update and arrange a date for the survey. It was a landline number as I recall, and was answered by a man who told me she herself was now deceased. So sad, both of them passed away…"

"It is, it is, ah, if you don't mind me asking, did you

speak to the man for long?"

"Not really, I updated him about the survey situation, gave him the good news that as they suspected planning permission would have to be delayed until the investigation was complete, and only then did he tell me he was not the Arthur Smith who had submitted the request with Ms. Briggs. I admit, I had made the assumption they resided at the same address. So, I told him I'd message Mr. Smith directly at the email address provided in their application, given that the case was time sensitive as the buildings were targeted to be demolished."

"Which day was this, if you don't mind me asking?" Daisy's stomach was a hard ball of knots now and she felt decidedly sick.

There was a pause as the woman on the other end scanned the notes on her computer, "That would be July fourth."

The day before Arthur was killed, Daisy tried to calm the trembling in her hand as she asked one final question, "And who was it that you spoke to?"

"Are you okay, Daisy? You look like you've seen a

ghost," Sylvia remarked as the vicar made her way slowly back into the kitchen. The start of a migraine pulsed at her left temple and Daisy couldn't face even the smallest bite from the plate of food in front of her.

"Um, not really, Sylvia, not really, bad headache – just done too much, I think," another white lie, but Daisy didn't want to share her findings with anyone other than the police. She couldn't chance the murderer catching on and targeting another victim. But then, could she guarantee Michelle Matlock would take her seriously? Would it perhaps not be better to confront the guilty party publicly and have the nice Detective Cluero as back up so they couldn't wriggle out of the accusation? The options churned through Daisy's mind on repeat until she could no longer make sense of any of it.

Prayer was needed, Daisy decided, and needed fast.

20. BATS IN THE BELFRY

News that they were being summoned to a public consultation in the parish hall at very little notice didn't go down well with the more distinguished members of the community, who muttered and whinged their way to their seats. The regular townsfolk, though, keen to be included in any business relating to Lillymouth and also nosey as to what this was all about, hurried in chattering happily.

The parish council took their seats on the small, raised platform, as befitted their status, with faces as hard as stone at the new vicar's impertinence at having gone over their heads and arranged this meeting in the first place. Daisy cared not. She stood at the front, bolstered by the encouraging faces of Sylvia and Joe, Bea and

Andrew, and even Rob Briggs, who seemed much happier to be there than his father up front. Gemma and Paul Dalton sat anxiously on the third row back, in the dark as much as everyone else as to why the vicar had called the meeting in the first place.

Daisy felt another wave of guilt as she considered the effect her news would have on those in the town who had been relying on the new development, not least Bea and Andrew, and not for the first time she wondered if she should simply focus on the murders and not on their root cause. To ignore the proposed projects up at Briggs' farm would be to ignore the motive altogether, though, as the development and the killing went hand in hand, so once again Daisy convinced herself to stick to her plan. Should she have confided in someone, though? Talked it through perhaps? Daisy was ruminating on this as the hall filled up, until she was pulled from her thoughts by the looming frame of Gerald Bunch towering over her.

"Ah, Mr. Bunch, there are free seats near the back I think," Daisy said dismissively.

"Quite so, quite so, I just realised I had not welcomed you to the parish properly," the man said, producing a ridiculously large bouquet from behind his back with a flourish, "with a gift."

"Oh, I'm not sure this is the time…" Daisy began, until forced to stop short as the mammoth, fragrant bunch was thrust into her arms, causing the vicar to almost lose her balance.

Of course, this gave Gerald Bunch the perfect opportunity to grab Daisy's elbow and help her carry the vibrant florals to a nearby table, brushing against her side as he did so. As soon as the flowers had been deposited none-too-gently, Daisy swapped her stick into the hand nearest the man, thus forcing some distance between the pair. Bunch must surely have noticed the obvious slight. Not only did he say nothing, however, but the smile on the man's thin face also never faltered. He simply gave a mock bow and slowly retreated, leaving Daisy rather hot under the dog collar – for all the wrong reasons.

If they hadn't been before, all eyes in the place were now firmly set on the new vicar and a general whispering had begun, no doubt debating whether she was in a relationship with the odious man. Daisy took a deep breath and decided it was now or never.

"Friends, neighbours," Daisy raised her voice over the general hubbub in the room, "residents of Lillymouth, thank you all for coming at such very short notice. I'll get straight to the point of the meeting. I'm sure you will be aware by now of the proposed developments up at Briggs' Farm, soon to be known as Briggs' Resort if Mr. Briggs Senior has his way," Daisy caught the eye of the man in question, ensconced on the stage with his cronies and so far looking casually relaxed, leaning back with one leg crossed over the other, and hurried on, "what you may not be aware of, however, is that the chance to formally voice your concerns on this project runs out in two days' time."

"That can't be right," Paul Dalton shouted out, "we haven't seen any public announcement from the planning department yet."

"That would be because the advisory notices were buried where very few would spot them," Daisy said calmly.

"But we still have time to object?" Gemma rubbed her husband's arm.

"You do," Daisy confirmed, "though further information has also come to light for us all to consider."

"I didn't realise the new lady vicar had been installed as mayor of the town," Robert Briggs Senior said mockingly, drawing out the term 'lady' as if it were a dirty word.

"Yes, far too big for her ugly boots," Violet Glendinning added scathingly, looking pointedly at Daisy's Doc Martens.

"Dad," Rob Briggs cautioned from the front row, "if the changes on our land are to go ahead, everything needs to be clear and above board, let Daisy speak." He gave the vicar a warm smile, which Daisy returned with a grateful nod.

"Don't be naïve!" Briggs Senior muttered in his son's direction, as Daisy spoke up again.

"Yes, ah, I have found evidence to suggest that there are, or may be, bats roosting in some of the buildings that would be demolished under the new plans. Given that it is illegal to remove roosts, even if there are no bats currently present, a survey needs to be conducted before planning permission can be considered."

"Rubbish!" Briggs Senior scoffed, "those barns have been unused for years now."

"Exactly, all the more ideal for wildlife," another resident piped up from near the back.

"It was, in fact, our late neighbour Arthur Smith who discovered this information, in collaboration with Mr. Briggs own sister, Lizzie, bless her soul," Daisy continued, her voice beginning to shake now she knew what must come. "Two dear friends who are no longer with us. A coincidence? I personally do not think so."

"What? You would bring our Lizzie into this?" Briggs bellowed from the makeshift stage, jumping to his feet and lurching forwards. It took two other members of the parish council to restrain him, though he kept up his tirade, "She was a sweet, dependable woman, not an ounce of bother until that man Smith got his dirty paws on her."

Daisy let the man rail and rant, aware that he wasn't doing himself any favours. He stopped short of outright blaming Arthur for Lizzie's death, but the implication was there.

"I thought Lizzie fell from the cliffs?" Uncle Joe spoke solemnly, his words directed at Briggs, for whom he had always harboured a strong dislike, "And yet now you imply she was pushed? And by the man she loved and who loved her? We all saw them about the town, besotted with each other they were. You're a fool if you think anyone will believe that version of events."

"Quite so," Sylvia agreed, "and that still wouldn't explain what happened to poor Arthur. Would you have us entertain the notion that the distraught man killed himself because he felt so guilty for murdering

Lizzie? Rubbish!"

"Well, you said it, not I!" Briggs roared, his bulbous eyes flashing hatred at everyone they landed on.

Daisy took a deep breath and tried to continue, though the din in the room meant she was not heard.

"Let the vicar speak!" The deep rasp of Gerald Bunch came from the back of the room, so loud that everyone was immediately silenced.

"Ah, thank you, Mr. Bunch," Daisy said quietly, "I actually have a theory of my own that I would like to share." She looked around the room, at the attentive faces of those assembled, pausing at her friend Bea – who now had a look of hurt and betrayal on her face – then onto Rob beside her on the front row and to the parish council on the stage, landing lastly on Robert Briggs. His friends had managed to get the man to sit back down, but his hands remained fisted and his face was a violent shade of purple.

Daisy's stomach rolled and gurgled, and she sent a silent prayer heavenwards.

"I have spoken to an organisation who do the bat surveys. They had already been contacted by Lizzie and Arthur with the evidence they had collected, but sadly both had passed away by the time the experts were ready to begin their survey. The day before Arthur's death, a representative of this organisation phoned Briggs' farm to speak to Lizzie. Upon hearing of her untimely death, they spoke to Robert Briggs, thinking he was Arthur. Tragically, I think this was the phone call which signed poor Arthur's death warrant, as by lunchtime the next day he had been dispatched back to our Maker. Our dear departed Nora Clumping was then pushed down the stairs at the vicarage after interrupting an intruder who had been searching Arthur's room – no doubt for copies of the evidence the bat society spoke of," a collective gasp echoed around the hall, as Daisy realised the parishioners had thought Nora simply died from old age, "Lizzie, well I can't be sure about her death, but I would suspect she challenged her brother and, owning half of the farm, refused to agree to his plans, thus setting the wheels in motion for her own demise, also at the hands of Robert Briggs here."

"You would accuse me? So publicly? It's slander! That's what it is. Lies, all of it! You've got bats in the belfry, vicar, anyone can see that, so obsessed still with your own grandmother's murder that you see guilt everywh…"

"Don't you dare bring Wendy into this," Joe jumped to